Southern
Belle's
Special
Gift

Other Books in the Keystone Stables Series

A Horse to Love (Book One)
On the Victory Trail (Book Two)
Summer Camp Adventure (Book Four)
Leading the Way (Book Five)
Blue Ribbon Champ (Book Six)
Whispering Hope (Book Seven)
The Long Ride Home (Book Eight)

Southern Belle's Special Gift

BOOK 3

KEYSTONE
Stables

Formerly titled *Trouble Times Two*

····• Marsha Hubler •····

ZONDERkidz

ZONDERVAN.com/
AUTHORTRACKER
follow your favorite authors

Zonderkidz

Southern Belle's Special Gift
Formerly titled *Trouble Times Two*
Copyright © 2005, 2009 by Marsha Hubler

Requests for information should be addressed to:
Zonderkidz, *Grand Rapids, MI 49530*

Library of Congress Cataloging-in-Publication Data

Hubler, Marsha, 1947-
   [Trouble times two]
   Southern Belle's special gift / Marsha Hubler.
      p. cm. (Keystone Stables ; bk. 3)
   Summary: Skye and Morgan have their hands full trying to share friendship and God's love with Tanya, a new foster child in the Chambers' household, who is a veteran shoplifter and a runaway but who shows surprising devotion to a mare and her foal.
   ISBN 978-0-310-71794-2 (softcover)
   [1. Horses—Fiction. 2. Foster home care—Fiction. 3. Christian life—Fiction. 4. Runaways—Fiction. 5. African Americans—Fiction. 6. Pennsylvania—Fiction.]
I. Title.
   PZ7.H86325So 2009
   [Fic]—dc22
                              2009001809

Interior illustrator: Lyn Boyer
Interior design and composition: Carlos Estrada and Sherri L. Hoffman

Printed in the United States of America

*Dedicated to the Susquehanna Valley Writers' Group
in Selinsgrove, Pennsylvania.*

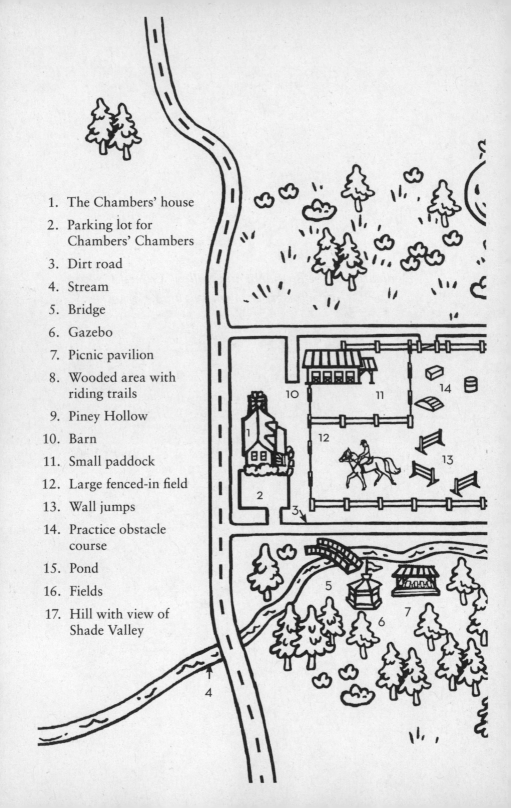

1. The Chambers' house

2. Parking lot for Chambers' Chambers

3. Dirt road

4. Stream

5. Bridge

6. Gazebo

7. Picnic pavilion

8. Wooded area with riding trails

9. Piney Hollow

10. Barn

11. Small paddock

12. Large fenced-in field

13. Wall jumps

14. Practice obstacle course

15. Pond

16. Fields

17. Hill with view of Shade Valley

Map of the Chambers' Ranch

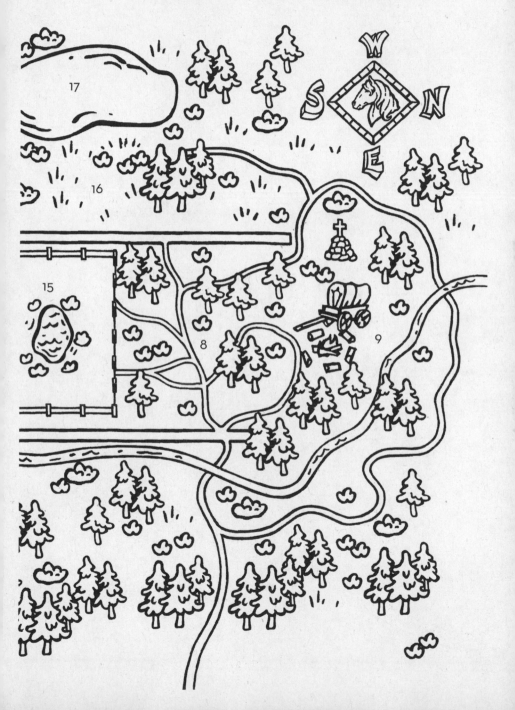

"Whoa, Champ! Easy fella!" Skye yelled. In his stall, the sorrel Quarter Horse pranced in place and then shuffled from side to side. Blasts of air snorted from his nose into the cold night like steam from a racing locomotive.

Skye rushed into the stall, her thick woolen mittens grabbing at his halter. She planted her boots firmly in the straw and struggled to control the powerful animal with all the strength she had in her slender frame.

Despite the cold, the quarter horse quivered in a slick coat of lather. His wild eyes searched every corner of the stall. Fear exploded from him and lodged in Skye's pounding heart. Horses can sense danger, and Skye knew he was sensing it now!

Odors of fresh manure and horse sweat were strong in the frigid January air. The barn echoed with the whinnies and stomps of five other frightened horses. Gusts of wind rattled the tin roof, heightening their fears.

"Easy, Blaze, easy!" a voice yelled from another part of the barn.

Skye released Champ's halter and hurried out of the stall, spinning toward the voice. Morgan sat in her wheelchair at the end of the stall—gloves raised, panic radiating from her freckled face. Behind a wire-mesh door, a dun mare pranced and snorted.

"Morgan," Skye yelled, "we better call Dad down here. I've never seen the horses get this stirred up over a little wind. Could be a bear or cougar prowling in the woods close by. You call Dad, and I'll try to quiet them down!"

Morgan motored her wheelchair past the racket toward the barn office. "You're right! They haven't been this bad since that big thunderstorm last summer. Be back in a sec!"

Skye stepped back into the stall and took hold of her horse's halter with both hands. "Easy, boy!" she coaxed.

Champ quickly settled into a calmer series of side-steps, head bobs, and trusting nickers. Skye stroked his arched neck, while her eyes checked the rest of his body for cuts or bruises. She grabbed a lead rope from a wall hook, clipped it to Champ's halter, and secured him to an iron bracket in the corner. "You're okay, boy," she assured him with firm pats on his chest. "I'm here."

Champ's ears, still twitching, pitched toward Skye. Eyes roving, searching—at last he stood firm. His muscles relaxed, he nickered softly, and then he nudged his muzzle into Skye's waiting embrace.

"That's better," Skye said, wrapping her arms around his neck and planting a kiss on his scratchy cheek. "Now take it easy. When the others are calmed down, I'll come back with your supper. And you'll need your blanket for a while. The way you're lathered up you could catch pneumonia in this cold night air."

Skye hurried to the next stall where a large black Tennessee Walker stomped and snorted. "Easy, Stormy," she said as she reached for the latch on the door. Then suddenly she stopped—her arm suspended in midair.

What was that? Had she heard something amid all the commotion? Or was the storm playing tricks on her?

"Skye! Skye Nicholson!"

Skye's brown eyes flashed. She turned and swept her long dark hair off her face, and then stopped, straining to listen past the noise around her.

"Over here!" The voice seemed to be coming from the tack room.

Skye spun around. There—in the doorway, in the shadows—was that someone peeking out? A face with an earring sparkling on each side?

Skye inched toward the doorway. "Who's there?" she called out uncertainly.

"It's me, Tanya!" a quivering voice answered. A tall African-American teenager stepped into the doorway, now in full view of the overhead lights. The girl folded her arms in a futile attempt to keep warm, her shapely frame covered with just a thin denim jacket and jeans. Her short ponytail and long strands of ringlets in front of her ears quivered as she tried to keep warm.

Skye stopped, her face frozen with surprise. "Tanya? Tanya Bell? But—when—how'd you get here?"

"I split from home!" Tanya piped above the commotion in the barn.

"C'mere—out into the open—where the horses can see you!" Skye angrily waved Tanya toward her. "No wonder they're so wound up. They picked up the scent of a stranger, but they couldn't see you."

"Their noses work that well? I was wondering why they were going nuts!" Tanya said as she joined Skye.

"Yeah, but they need to put a body with the scent. C'mere." Skye tugged the girl's sleeve. "We've got to settle them down."

"Mr. C. will be right—" Morgan yelled as she came around the corner, "Hey ... what's goin' on? And who's this?"

"In a sec," Skye said, pulling Tanya with her. "Follow me. I want you to stick your hand out as we go to each stall. Let the horses get a good whiff. When they can smell you and see you, we'll have some peace."

Cautiously, the two girls approached each stall. Skye "horse-talked" while Tanya forced her hand out as though she were sticking it in a bucket of manure. Six stalls later, a relaxed chorus of nickering horses voiced their impatience for their oats and hay.

"So this is what made them go off the deep end!" Morgan said, joining the girls. "Like I said before—who are you? And where did you drop in from?"

"Okay, Tanya. Let's hear it," Skye added. "How'd you get here from the Millers? You are staying in town with the Millers, aren't you? Oh, sorry, Morgan. This is Tanya Bell. I met her last summer at the county fair."

"Hi. I'm Morgan Hendricks." Morgan brushed her red hair back and studied Tanya's tall, slender frame. "So, what are you doing in our barn at this time of night anyway?"

Tanya smacked a large wad of gum and blew a bubble until it popped.

"Tanya!" Skye said sharply. "No bubbles in here, or the horses will go nuts again!"

"Oh, sorry," Tanya answered curtly. Her hands made their way into her jeans pockets. "I took a bus from Philly to the mall down the road. Then I met a truck driver who just happened to be driving past Keystone, and ta dah! Here I am!"

"Are you crazy?" Morgan recoiled. "It's gotta be hundreds of miles from Philadelphia to the mall! Then you hitched a ride with a stranger? Do you know how dangerous that is?"

"And—do your parents know you're here?" Skye asked. "Where are you headed? To the Millers'?"

"Who are the Millers?" Morgan lifted her hands in frustration.

"Well ... I was going to the Millers' place—Barb Miller's my aunt—she lives in town. I've spent a lot of time with her and Uncle Frank," Tanya said. "But when I called their house from the mall, their dog sitter answered. Turns out Aunt Barb and Uncle Frank are in Florida for a month. Go figure. So I decided to come out here. I just had to get away from home. I needed time to think."

"You couldn't think in Philly?" Skye released a sarcastic jab.

A large steel door slid open behind the girls.

"No critters out there tonight!" A man in a cowboy hat and heavy woolen coat hurried through the doorway, a spotlight the size of a basketball nestled in his thick leather gloves. "Must be—"

Mr. Chambers looked up just then and stood stock still, a look of confusion sweeping over his wind-burned face. "Ah—now wait a minute. Two girls headed to this barn twenty minutes ago, and now I see one—two—three. Clue me in, girls," he said. He shoved the spotlight under his arm and drew his gloved hand down over his brown mustache.

"This is a friend of mine," Skye answered, pulling the girl closer by her sleeve. "She—ah—kinda ran away from home."

"Kinda?" Mr. Chambers walked slowly toward the girls.

Morgan swung her chair around. "We've got six hungry horse tummies crying the blues. I'll get started with their oats. Later, guys." She grabbed a pail and headed toward Blaze's stall.

Tanya took another step backward, started to blow a bubble, but then changed her mind. "I'm Tanya Bell, and, okay, I didn't *kinda* run away. I big-time ran away. I live in Philly."

13

"I see," Mr. Chambers said as if he found runaway girls from Philly in his barn every night. "Well, I think the first thing we need to do is go up to the house and call your folks. They're probably worried to death, wondering where you are. Let's go, ladies. Morgan, are you okay here?"

"Sure thing!" Morgan yelled back from Blaze's stall.

Skye reached behind her, grabbing Tanya's cold hand. "Come on," she said. "Everything will be fine."

chapter two

The next week, Skye found herself with Mr. and Mrs. Chambers, Morgan, and Tanya in a humongous den at Tanya's home. They sat in silence in an arc of marshmallowy sofas embedded in a thick, lush carpet. With her back to the group, an African-American woman in a teal pantsuit stared at a stone fireplace which covered the entire wall.

"Tanya, I simply can't believe you were shoplifting again!" The woman spun around, disappointment draping over her like a dark veil. "And then on top of that, you ran away from us—from everything you have here!" She stared pitchforks at Tanya before turning away to pick up a poker and jab at the fire. The burning wood crackled and sent up a barrage of sparks. The woman's soft black hair hung freely from her teal blue headband and bounced off the top of her shoulders. Sparkling gold teardrop earrings dangled from her ears and jostled with her hair.

Skye shifted her attention to a wall that looked like a glass checkerboard. Beyond the windows, she could see a cozy patio and swimming pool covered with a layer of snow. *Wow!* Skye thought. *She ran away from this?*

Skye's stare returned to the den. During the woman's entire tirade, Tanya sat playing with her long fingernails that were painted red with silver sparkles.

"Mother, it had nothing to do with you and Father. I just needed time to think. I needed some space," Tanya answered curtly without looking up.

"Well, it seems to me you have all the space you need right here. Or isn't that bedroom big enough for you? How much space do you need, young lady?" the woman responded with a jab of sarcasm.

Tanya settled deeper into the sofa, crossed her legs with a jolt, and studied her nails. She gave one long, deep, bored sigh.

"Please mind your manners." Dr. Bell's smooth bronze face frowned. Dark brown eyes flashed their disapproval below long curly lashes.

"Dr. Bell," Mrs. Chambers said, "it's obvious Tanya has some issues that might need extra help. Her stacking up a court record of misdemeanors is certainly not a reflection of your and your husband's parenting skills. From what you've told us, it sounds like Tanya has some deep-rooted problems."

"Isn't that ironic?" Dr. Bell put down the poker and sat next to her daughter. "I'm a gynecologist, a specialist for women and girls, but I can't help this girl." The anger on her face melted into deep concern. "I still can't believe she shoplifted again. The last time she promised us—she promised us!—that she would never do it again. Tanya, you have everything. What was that head of yours thinking?"

"Mother, I did it—just because!"

"Just because? That's it? Just because?"

"Dr. Bell, at least Tanya has come clean." Mr. Chambers leaned his elbows on his knees and folded his hands. "If she hadn't, you'd be tied up in court proceedings for months, and I think this time the judge would've shown no mercy. The surveillance camera at the mall caught the whole thing. Tanya's admitting the crime and returning the stolen jewelry is a big step in the right direction. Now we need to act quickly to get her the help she needs."

Gently, Dr. Bell placed her ring-covered fingers on Tanya's knee, and her eyes begged Tanya to look at her. "Lord knows how hard it's been for this dear child to cope with losing her mother. When Mariam died, Tanya lived with her aunt and her grandmother, but she might as well have been a foster child. They bounced her around like a rubber ball between the two of them. I could tell when they came to me for checkups that this little girl just wasn't happy. That's when we decided we wanted to adopt her. It's been ten years now.

"I've known Tanya since she was born. In fact, I was there when she was born! Roger loves her dearly, too, but he's away so much on business trips, he just can't give her a lot of time. He's on the west coast right now."

She's adopted? Skye thought. She and Morgan exchanged peaked eyebrows. *Wow!*

"Hey, the Chambers are trying to adopt me!" Morgan said.

"Yeah, me too!" Skye added with a big smile.

Dr. Bell continued, "Well, I'm certainly glad to hear that. I've seen enough of the foster care system to make my blood boil. But sending Tanya so far away for a whole year—it seems so drastic. Roger and I are very concerned about her education. Transferring from a private academy to a public school can be traumatic for a teenager. She's a straight A student. On the other hand, you obviously seem to care deeply about the children who are staying with you. Exactly what kind of foster home do you have?"

"It's called Keystone Stables," Skye bubbled, "and it's a neat place for all kinds of kids! We have horses, a pond, a game room—everything! I've been there about a year, and the Chambers really helped me get my act together. I was, like, a rotten know-it-all before I lived with them. And then, even though Judge Mitchell was ready to ship me to Chesterfield, he let me live with the Chambers."

"What's Chesterfield?" Dr. Bell asked.

"It's a detention center in northeastern Pennsylvania," Mrs. Chambers said. "More of a lockdown for kids who have a hard time following rules." Her smile and blue eyes lit up the room.

Tanya sat completely engrossed in her nails. She yawned obnoxiously.

Morgan beamed as she flipped her long hair behind her shoulders. "You won't be sorry if Tanya comes to live with us. Keystone is really different."

"It's not like any foster home I've ever been in," Skye said, "and I've been in lots. Mom and Dad really do care about us. I learned that the hard way."

Dr. Bell forced a smile. "I see."

Mr. Chambers looked at his watch and then stood. "Well, Dr. Bell, I hate to rush this, but we need to get going. We have a four-hour drive ahead of us. I know you have a tremendous amount of apprehension, but, I assure you, Tanya will get the best of care. You and Mr. Bell's decision to grant us custody went a long way with the judge. I want to personally thank you for helping us financially. And don't worry about Tanya's education. Madison Middle School is a fine school. It's rated as one of the best in the state. Now, if you're willing to sign the papers, Tanya can finish packing, and we'll be on our way. As soon as you and your husband get a break in your schedule, please come to visit."

"We surely will—the first chance we get."

Tanya jumped up from her seat and headed toward a long flight of stairs that led to an open loft on the second floor. "I'm going to check my room once more. I'll be ready in five minutes."

At Keystone Stables, two days and one trip to the mall later, Skye and Morgan decided to drop into Tanya's room "uninvited."

"I wanna see what money can do for a bedroom that's been crying for a face-lift," Skye whispered as she and Morgan headed down the hallway. Behind them came Tippy and Tyler, the Chambers' West Highland terriers, clicking their nails on the hardwood floor.

"Hey," Morgan called, knocking on the closed door, "anybody home?"

The door squeaked open an inch, and a brown eyeball peeked through the crack. "What?" Tanya said.

"C'mon, Tanya," Skye said, "only bears hibernate in winter. We wanna see your room."

"There's nothing to see," Tanya answered coldly.

"Yeah, right," Skye said, "like, you're livin' in a jail cell. I saw all the bags you and Mom carried in from the car. C'mon, let's see."

"Tsk, children!" Skye heard grumbling from behind the door that opened like it was guarding a sacred tomb. "But the dogs stay out!" she blasted loudly from the room.

"Sorry, fellas," Morgan said to the dogs, "not in this room."

The dogs turned and walked down the hall.

"Maybe we should take our shoes off," Skye whispered to Morgan. The girls snickered as they cautiously entered the room.

Tanya made her way to the far wall where she had already started arranging books on top of a desk. The bed had teddy bears of all sizes and colors sitting at every post. The corners of the room were cluttered with paperback books stacked several feet high. Tanya moved from the desk to the windows and busied herself fluffing

19

the lace curtains. She deliberately had her back to the visitors.

Morgan parked at the side of the bed, and Skye flopped across the fluffy new bedspread trimmed with fancy lilac-colored lace. Bears flew everywhere!

"P-l-e-a-s-e!" Tanya spun around and griped like a grumpy librarian. "I spent hours fixing this dinky room! Go flop in your own rooms! In here, you sit softly, if you don't mind. This pathetic hole might only be a pittance of my own bedroom, but it will be neat. Now pick those bears up off the floor. " She hurried to the bed and painstakingly rearranged every bear.

"Duh—excuse me!" Skye yawned, taking her time picking up a few bears from the floor. Tossing them on the bed, she slid cautiously onto the edge. "Hey, we barely know you, and you can hardly bear us!" she said with a chuckle.

"Skye, you are too funny!" Morgan giggled so hard she held her sides.

Skye felt her face flush. She placed her hands over her mouth to suppress the string of giggles locked inside. Finally, her snicker exploded.

"V-e-r-y funny." A stingy smile escaped from Tanya's lips. "I should think that one of the ridiculous rules of this place would be to respect other people's property. I'm sure I heard that somewhere in that list Mr. Chambers read last night. Boring!" Like a queen at her throne, Tanya sat on a padded chair next to the desk, watching every move the visitors made.

"Hey, it was your idea to come here," Skye said. Without thinking, she picked up a fuzzy blue bear, and Tanya glared holes through her. Back down on the bed the bear went. "Besides, everybody has rules. We probably have a few zillion more because Keystone is licensed by the state and has regulations—and horses."

"Yeah," Morgan agreed. "Our safety is important to Mr. and Mrs. C. They're also into our homework and test scores in school—big time."

Tanya's eyes focused on Morgan's wheelchair. "Hey, I've been wanting to know how come you're in that thing."

"Cerebral palsy," Morgan answered, "and it's not a thing. It's a Jazzy, and I do just fine in this thing, thank you. Hey Tanya, how do you feel about starting at Madison next Monday? I mean, that's a little red schoolhouse compared to your fancy academy in Philly. And what are you doing with all these books?" Her glance swept the room.

"Hello! I read them," Tanya sassed. "What do you do with your books? Make paper airplanes? Use them as firewood? As soon as the man puts my shelves together, these books will be lined up in alphabetical order and ready for business. I brought only my favorites with me. I still have hundreds at home."

Skye surveyed the room and decided there were hundreds in this room as well. "So that's what you've been doin' the last two days. And, duh, of course we read books, but not by the dozens. You must really, really like to read. And just in case you're interested, I think there are about 120 kids in your eighth grade at Madison. Oh, and one of them is Robin Ward. You just gotta meet her. She's too cool."

Tanya busied herself rearranging the books on the desk. "At Ridgecrest Academy I had only a few choice friends. It depends on what your hang-ups are, and the things you like and all that get you together with other kids. I'll clue you in right now. Winning the Miss Friendship Award is not one of my goals at Madison. I have other things to occupy my mind. Nine times out of ten, I choose to spend time with me. I have my books and mp3 player—well—just my books here. How do you cope with not listening to rock and rap? I'll go out of my mind!"

"Like, that's it? Reading?" asked Skye. "Don't you have any hobbies? Like sports or playing an instrument or—yeah, like riding horses? You're living with some now, just in case you haven't noticed."

"I hate horses! They stink! I hope I never have to go near them again," Tanya complained.

"Oh, this oughta be real good," Skye said. "You're living at Keystone Stables, and you don't wanna be near horses? Tanya, something tells me your brain was in smarts withdrawal. Everybody who lives here learns to ride—and helps with barn chores."

"Not me! They can't make me," Tanya smarted off. "Trust me! My mother will stop it. All I have to do is cry in front of her."

"Well, we'll just see," Skye informed her.

"'Why don't you like horses?" Morgan asked.

"Man, you guys are nosy. What is this, the third degree?" Tanya stood, shoved the chair sharply against the desk, hurried to the door, and then flung it open. "Just leave me alone!"

chapter three

Saturday afternoon, between Tanya's griping about the food and the size of her "pathetic" room, Skye managed to show her the rest of Keystone Stables. Although a touch of fresh snow was swirling and dancing with the wind, the sun in the deep blue sky helped thaw things out enough for the girls to go on a short tour on the four-wheeler.

The girls wrapped up in clothes that easily would have taken them to the top of Mount Everest. Moving like starched dolls, they put helmets and goggles on. Skye promised, promised, promised to drive slowly and safely. Tanya griped her way onto the back of the four-wheeler, and they took off down the road along the fenced pasture. Skye showed her the picnic grove, trails through the woods, Piney Hollow, and the magnificent view of Shade Valley from the hill behind the barn. In about a half hour, they pulled up in front of the barn, their faces fiery red from the cutting wind.

Tanya slid off the four-wheeler and yanked off her helmet. "No swimming pool! What do you do all summer? Play in traffic?"

"Tanya, just take it easy, okay?" Skye snapped. She took off her helmet, hanging it and Tanya's on the handlebars. A wisp of wind played with Skye's hair, forcing her to control the long strands with her hands, then she leaned back against the four-wheeler seat. "You're not even here a week, and you've griped about anything and everything. It's gonna be a long, lousy year if you don't find something that you can crack a smile about. There's lots to do around here, especially in the summer. We have picnics and the horses—oh, yeah, you aren't into them. And we can swim in the pond. Then there's the Snyder County Fair with its cool horse show. You already know about that from living with your aunt."

"Swimming in that dirty old hole?" Tanya pointed to the bottom of the field. "You'll see me ride a horse first! Picnics? This city girl can hardly wait."

"Exactly what did you expect to find here? The Taj Mahal? This is country, girl. We get out lots during the week. There's church, the mall, and—hey, we do have a library in town."

Tanya snickered, took off her goggles, and hung them with her helmet. "Library, yeah, right. It's about as big as my bedroom."

"How about the Barnes and Noble behind the mall?"

"Yeah, I remember that." Tanya cracked a weak smile. "Now we're talking. At least I can get my hands on some decent books. And one more thing. Tell me I didn't hear you say church."

"Yep. We go every Sunday, and it's so cool. Our teen group is called 'Youth for Truth,' and we do all kinds of neat things. We have pizza parties, go bowling, and once a month everybody comes here to our game room. We go on trips and have retreats a few times a year. Now there's a bunch of really cool kids. Robin's in the group, and Melissa Richards, and Chad Dressler!" Skye's face flared hot despite the frigid wind.

24

Tanya shivered, pulled her hood up, and buttoned it around her head. "Aw, stuff like that doesn't interest me in the least. And church? I can take it or leave it. My real gram used to take me when I was a kid, but I haven't been there since Mother and Father adopted me. They're too busy with work and all. Just give me a couple good books and a room like a tomb, and I'm happy. Of course, now and then, I do like a good party. You know what I mean, Skye?" Tanya bounced her eyebrows.

Skye took her goggles off and hung them on the handle-bars. "This wind's turning me into an ice cube. Let's go into the barn. It's chore time anyway. And remember, no bubble popping or shouting in there. It spooks the horses. As far as partying goes, your kind of parties won't fly around here."

"But I'm not dumb enough to get caught."

Skye started toward the barn. "Tanya, don't be stupid. You can't pull anything like that around here. Mom and Dad have eyes in the back of their heads. And Mom's called The Bloodhound at Maranatha. She can sniff out trouble like Deputy Dawg on a bunny trail. By the way, don't forget about Maranatha. You'll have counseling there after school every day. Mom and the other counselors know how to get inside your head, so you might as well spill the beans as soon as you show your face. It's a lot less painful. They probably know exactly why you've been lifting all that stuff, even if you don't."

"There's no reason," Tanya said, following Skye into the barn. "I just do it."

"There's got to be a reason. There's a reason for everything we do—good or bad. Which brings me to the reason why we have chores to do in the barn."

"Skye, I told you I'm not doing any chores around these stinking horses, so you can forget it."

"Then you're gonna get g-r-o-u-n-d-e-d, big time!"

25

"That will fit into my life like the last piece of an awesome puzzle," Tanya said, sneering. "Grounded from what? Watching the grass grow? I can't think of anything better than hiding in my bedroom with all my favorite books. Let them ground me!"

Skye grabbed a pitchfork off the barn wall and shoved the handle into Tanya's arms. "Here! Hold that!" she said sharply. "I need to get the wheelbarrow! Tell me one thing, Tanya. Why did you come here anyway?"

"I needed time to think," she said smugly.

"Looks like you're gonna think yourself into stone," Skye said as she grabbed a wheelbarrow from one corner. She took the pitchfork from Tanya and laid it across the wheelbarrow. "Anyway, let me show you the horses, one by one. Maybe one of them will wink at you the right way. And let me tell you loud and clear, you will learn to ride one. It probably won't be until spring when all the snow is gone, but as sure as you can read, you will learn to ride."

"We'll just see," Tanya spewed out.

"Yeah, we'll just see all right," Skye said. She gave Tanya the horse tour of her life, starting with Skye's pride and joy, Champ. Visiting five other stalls, Skye pulled Tanya by her coat sleeve to the half-open Dutch doors and introduced each horse. Tanya refused to touch the animals or even step close. She tsked until Skye thought Tanya's tongue would tsk out of her mouth. At the sixth stall, a dark reddish-brown horse with a white strip on its face popped its head out and whinnied. Tanya jumped back like she had been struck by lightning. "I'm outta here!" she said, backing away. "That noise grosses me out."

"C'mere, silly," Skye said. "She's only saying hi. There's something really special about this horse. Did you ever see a pregnant one?"

"Pregnant?" Tanya squeaked out and took one step forward. "I never thought of horses being pregnant. Hmm, I guess they're not hatched from eggs, are they?"

Skye giggled and pulled Tanya closer. "Not hardly. This is Southern Belle, our chestnut Morgan mare. Dad got her at auction a couple months ago for a good price. Look at her tummy."

"Her name is Bell, like mine? Cool," Tanya took another cautious step forward. She peered into the stall, focusing on the mare's huge barrel. "Wow! She looks like she's ready to explode! I never knew horses got so big! And what does chestnut Morgan mean?"

The Bambi eyes of the horse studied Tanya intently. The horse pitched her ears forward, listening to the strange, new voice.

Skye stroked the soft, velvety nose. "Chestnut means she's a dark reddish brown with no black on her any-where. And Morgan means the kind of breed she is. A Morgan has a short stocky build and real thick neck. And right now, Belle has a real stocky build."

"Is she going to have twins or triplets? She's so big!"

"Nah, there's only one in there. Horses usually have only one at a time. She's gonna foal in May, the vet said. He's a little worried, though. He told Dad the other day that he didn't think Belle had good care before we got her. She was super underweight. She's starting to look half decent now, but the vet's still worried."

"Worried about what?" Tanya's voice expressed a budding concern.

"Well, that she or the foal might not make it. We've been giving her the best hay and oats, and all kinds of vitamins. Horses are the same as humans when it comes to needing the right food to have a healthy baby."

Skye's glance shifted to Tanya who stood entrenched in her thoughts. "Go on. Pet her," Skye said. "She won't bite."

Slowly, Tanya inched her hand toward Belle, who responded with an accepting nicker.

Tanya jumped back. Finally, her face covered in determination, she stretched two fingers forward and stroked the soft velvety nose as though it were made of glass. "She—she's beautiful," Tanya whispered. Then she pressed her entire hand on Belle's nose. "I'll take care of her," she suddenly announced. "She's got to make it. She's just got to."

chapter four

Mrs. Chambers, the three girls, and Tip and Ty had joined Mr. Chambers in the living room for evening devotions, which was an important part of the daily routine at Keystone Stables.

"Tanya, tell us a little about yourself," Mr. Chambers said, placing his open Bible on his lap. His brown mustache twitched as he smiled from ear to ear.

"There's nothing to tell," Tanya said with her head down. Sitting next to Skye on the sofa, Tanya super slumped and started another fingernail study. "I was born, Mom died, I lived with Gram and Aunt Barb, and now I live with the Bells. That's all. No big deal." She never looked up.

Mrs. Chambers opened her Bible and ruffled some pages. "Oh, but your life is a big deal, Tanya, especially to God. Listen to this wonderful verse from the book of John. 'I have come that they may have life, and have it to the full.' Do you know who said that?"

"Nope," Tanya muttered.

"Did Jesus say that?" Skye asked.

"Yes, he did. And, girls, the Bible tells us that God promises all of us eternal life with him if we trust Christ as our Savior. He wants to give us a life filled with peace and joy here on earth, even through tough times."

Tanya never looked away from her nails.

"I'm so glad I did that a few years ago," Morgan said. "I had zillions of hang-ups until I gave my life to God. Now he steers me down the right paths, no matter how rocky they are—even in this wheelchair!"

"Hey, I'm not into this religion stuff," Tanya informed everyone promptly. "Church? I can take it or leave it. I'd rather leave it."

Skye poked Tanya gently with her elbow. "I thought that too until I was in a truck accident. I woke up in the hospital and realized I could've been killed. Then I also realized I needed someone else in charge of my life. On my own, I had messed it up really bad."

Tanya went on staring at her nails.

"I accepted Christ right in the hospital that same night," Skye continued. "How sweet was that? I wasn't near a church. There wasn't even a preacher in the room!"

Mr. Chambers picked up his Bible. "Tanya, we're not talking about religion. Many verses in here tell us that being a Christian is having a loving relationship with Jesus Christ. It's not just going to church. Of course, once you accept Christ, church takes on a whole new meaning. Becoming a Christian begins with recognizing that God offers you the gift of salvation. You can't earn it. But you can receive it."

Tanya glanced at Mr. Chambers and then looked back at her nails. "Yeah, I kinda remember that stuff from Gram's church when I was little. But it's just not important to me anymore. I don't think God cares at all about me. If he did, he wouldn't have let my mom die."

Mrs. Chambers closed her Bible and looked up. Her blue eyes glistened. "Tanya, we're praying that while you live with us, you'll realize that God does love you. Sure, what happened to you was awful, and I know you've had a rough time. God's heart breaks along with yours and it doesn't end there. He hasn't given up. He has great plans for you and your life."

"Yeah," Skye said. "I never even knew my parents. I don't even have a clue where they are. But look at the neat parents God has given me."

Tanya said nothing.

"Next time we have devotions, we'll talk about God and what we should do when nasty things come our way," Mr. Chambers said. He closed his Bible and placed it on the stand next to a lamp. "Let's have a word of prayer, and then I want to discuss this week's major events."

They all bowed their heads. Skye noticed Tanya's eyes were wide open.

Mr. Chambers finished praying, smoothed his mustache, leaned back in his chair, and folded his arms. "Okay, girls," he said, "what's on the agenda this week?"

"Can I go to my room?" Tanya blurted out.

"We'd like you to stay just a few more minutes while we discuss the upcoming activities," Mrs. Chambers said. "You'll be a part of many of them. We like you girls to know exactly what's going on around here."

"Oh, all right!" Tanya snapped and crossed her arms.

"I, for one, am going to be very busy." Mr. Chambers sighed, his glance drifting upward. "I have three new orders for computer systems, and there are five crabby hard drives sitting in my office to repair. I also have three house calls to make—in addition to the barn chores. And, oh yes. This is very, very important. Wednesday night Doc Gonzales is coming to check on Southern Belle."

Tanya finally stared at Mr. Chambers, hanging on every word.

"And, hon," Mr. Chambers said, smiling at his wife, "didn't you say there's a parent-teacher fellowship at Madison this week?"

"Yeah, it's for my seventh grade," Skye said, her voice pitched with excitement. "It's Tuesday night. I have 4-H after school Wednesday, and Thursday our Youth for Truth group practices, doesn't it?"

"Right," Morgan said. "And I can't wait. My three years of flute lessons are finally paying off."

"Youth for Truth?" Tanya expressed slight interest.

Skye giggled and ran her hands through her hair. "This is nuts, but there are a few kids from our church youth group who come here every Thursday night to jam—some classical but mostly praise music. But it's all been rewritten with a faster tempo. Morgan and Robin play flutes, Bobby Noll plays the trumpet, Melissa Richards plays a clarinet, and Mrs. Chambers does her cool thing on that." Skye pointed to a digital piano in the corner. "Chad plays guitar." *Wonderful Chad*, Skye thought. "And—hold on now—I play the violin."

"Her lessons and long hours of practice are paying off," Mrs. Chambers added. "She doesn't do a half-bad job."

Tanya hung a smirk on her face that could have won first place in a National Smirk Contest. "Skye? The violin? Here at Keystone Stables, in the middle of nowhere?"

"Yes, me and the violin!" Skye announced loudly. "I've been taking lessons about a year, and it's awesome. My music teacher writes my parts over so they're not too hard for me to play. I love playing in the group. We're not that good, but it's a blast." *And Chad being here makes it all worthwhile!*

Mr. Chambers stood and yawned. "Don't laugh, Tanya. Violins are in right now. Something I'd think you would know if you're up on the latest 'cool' music. Isn't that right, dear?" he said passing his wife on his way to the kitchen. "Coffee time!"

"Definitely," Mrs. Chambers said. "And if you'd like, Tanya, you can join the group, although if I remember correctly, you've never taken music lessons of any kind, have you?"

"Nah, I'm not into that kind of stuff," Tanya answered.

Mrs. Chambers stood and headed toward the kitchen. "Do you girls want some iced tea or cocoa? We'll play some games in a few minutes—that is, if your homework's done."

"It is," Skye said. "Cocoa for me, please."

"Me, too," Morgan added.

"Now can I go?" Tanya said rudely as she jumped up from the sofa and hurried out of the room.

The new school year started at Madison with Skye and Morgan escorting their foster sister the first day. For the next week, Tanya fought everything the other two girls tried to do to make her transition easier. She sat alone on the bus and walked through the halls with her nose in the air, all the other kids avoiding her like the plague. Even Robin's first attempt at making friends with Tanya ended in failure. "She acts like some queen bee," Robin complained to Skye, "and I'm not gonna waste my time on her!"

"School is school!" That's all that came out of Tanya's mouth when anyone in the house asked her about starting at Madison. In addition to her refusing to discuss school, she made a beeline to the barn as soon as she got home from Maranatha. Her newfound interest in Belle had the rest of the family stumped. She asked Skye to show her how to pet the mare, brush her, and just plain love her. During chore time, Tanya was always the first one to the barn, without a single complaint.

Tanya willingly learned how to muck the stall and did it like she was cleaning her own bedroom. The floor almost sparkled before she spread fresh straw all around! Skye showed her how to feed and water properly, the exact amount of food and supplements recorded in a journal that Tanya carried with her. And when it came to grooming, there wasn't a shinier chestnut mare in Snyder County. Everyone agreed that Tanya's attachment to Belle was a God thing, a miracle. While Tanya lived at Keystone Stables, Belle would be Tanya's horse.

On Wednesday evening after supper, the whole family went to the barn to muck out stalls and feed and groom the horses. When the work was finished, Skye showed Tanya how to lead Belle to an open stall and cross tie her between two brackets on opposite walls. Skye watched while Tanya took her first clumsy turn cleaning each hoof with a hoof pick. Then the girls brushed Belle while they waited for Dr. Gonzales to arrive.

"Hello, Tom!" a deep voice yelled in the barn doorway.

"In here, Doc!" Mr. Chambers yelled, hurrying from one of the end stalls. "We've got her all ready for you."

A tall, thin Hispanic man wearing a bright red baseball cap and a dark green jump suit walked in from the darkness. Dirty rubber boots covered his legs up to his knees. Both arms were filled with bulging black bags. "I'm so glad the January thaw is here," he said, walking toward Belle. "December's weather wasn't fit for man or beast. I'm finally getting caught up on my house calls — or should I say barn calls." He gently set the two bags down, placed his hands on his hips, and stared at Belle from head to tail. "Well, she's looking a lot better than she did when I saw her last, Tom. Somebody must be giving her the Queen for the Day treatment. Every day!"

"Hi, Doc." Skye pointed to Tanya, still brushing her heart out. "Here's part of the reason. This is Tanya Bell from Philly. She's been taking care of Belle for the last few days."

Never turning around, Tanya continued to groom the horse. "Is she going to be all right?" she blurted out.

Mr. Chambers joined the group. "Whoa, Tanya, the doc will tell us soon enough," he said. "Let him do his exam first. Then we'll know a lot more."

Slowly Dr. Gonzales took several steps toward the horse. "Easy, now," he whispered and put his hand under Belle's muzzle. "Take a good whiff, girl. You've met me before. Now let's see how you and your baby are doing."

Mr. Chambers went to the front of the horse and clutched her halter. "Girls, I'd like you to step back now. Belle tends to get a little panicky when she realizes who's working on her. Some horses are just like kids. Give them a shot once, and they never forget it—or the one who gave it to them."

While Mr. Chambers held the horse's halter, Dr. Gonzales slowly smoothed his hand down over Belle's neck, across her back, and under her belly. Belle let out a soft nicker, nodded her head, and relaxed her back leg. "Good girl," the doctor said. "Getting used to me, I see."

Skye and Tanya stood behind Mr. Chambers, watching every move the doctor made.

Dr. Gonzales eased away from the mare, reached into one of his bags, and pulled out a stethoscope. He plugged it into his ears and eased himself close to Belle again. "Easy, girl. Now this won't hurt." Gently he placed the round end on the horse's distended barrel. He listened, slid the instrument around, and listened again, then he slipped to the other side and carefully repeated the procedure.

"What's he doing?" Tanya whispered.

"Listening for the baby's heartbeat," Skye answered. "Sh-h."

Dr. Gonzales inched his way to the front of the mare, placing the stethoscope on a half dozen places on her neck and chest. "Belle sounds a little better today, Tom. Her heartbeat is much stronger than it was during her last exam. I'm still concerned about the foal, though. That sonogram I took last month indicated an underdeveloped baby. The heartbeat is still pretty weak. I sure hope Belle can carry it at least eleven months. I don't want to see this foal any sooner than early May."

"Why? What's wrong?" Tanya blurted out.

Mr. Chambers stroked Belle's face with his gloved hand. "Tanya's kind of claimed Belle as her own, Doc. She's like an old mother hen with this horse."

"That's quite all right," the doctor said softly. He lifted Belle's upper lip and looked at her teeth. "This mare needs a lot of TLC right now. Young lady, you just might help both of them pull through."

"Pull through?" Tanya asked. "Is it that bad?"

Skye touched Tanya's arm. "Now don't get yourself all wound up in knots. She'll be okay."

"You have been pumpin' her full of all kinds of vitamins, haven't you, Tom?" the veterinarian asked. He stepped to his bag and pulled out a thermometer that looked like a fat pencil. He stepped to the mare's side, gently slid his hand over Belle's back, then lifted her tail and slid the thermometer inside her.

"Yes," Tom answered, still holding the halter tightly. "She's getting the best of everything we can afford. And now since Tanya's here, Belle has her own private nurse." His mustache twitched with his friendly smile.

"Now what's—" Tanya started to say.

"He's taking Belle's temperature," Skye interrupted. "I figured you'd wanna know that too. Horses don't get their temperature taken in their mouths like we do. They'd chomp the thermometer into a zillion pieces."

The doctor slowly pulled the thermometer out and read it. "A hundred flat! Well, that's as normal as normal can be. A good sign!" He stepped away from the mare and once more looked her over. A broad smile beamed from his face. "Well, despite the poor start both of them got, things seem to be shaping up. I look for a healthy foal in about four months. I had planned to do an internal today, but I think I'll wait another month. That'll give the baby a few more weeks to mature. By the end of February, we should know a lot more."

"They've got to make it," Tanya said. "They've just got to."

chapter five

That was great, kids," Mrs. Chambers said at the digital piano in her living room. The Youth for Truth music group sat in a circle behind her. "This ensemble is getting better every week. You'll soon be ready for Carnegie!" She smiled at the group, then turned a few pages in a large black binder that she had posted on her piano rack.

"Aw, Mrs. Chambers, we're not nearly that good." Robin Ward giggled, grasping the flute like the baseball bat she'd rather be swinging.

"Yeah," Skye said, her eyes riveted on Chad who sat on the sofa adjusting the strings on his guitar. "The only part of Carnegie we'll ever see will be from the auditorium seats, lookin' up. But this 'Jesu, Joy of Man's Desiring' is so cool. I never thought in a zillion years that I'd like anything Bach wrote."

Morgan held her flute with the same care she would a newborn baby. "There's so much awesome music that was written back then. You don't know how cool it is until you actually try to play it."

"Yeah," Bobby added. His chubby hand poked at wire-rimmed glasses that slid down on his nose. He wiped his hand over the top of his spiked brown hair, pretending to arrange it. "I like this kind of music, but maybe that's because my mother made me take lessons since I started breathing."

The room filled with giggles and snickers.

Bobby, you're so lame! Skye thought. Her glance bounced briefly to Bobby, then back to Chad.

"I've been taking lessons forever too," Chad said, his dark brown eyes highlighting his wavy blond hair. "But I've always loved music. Any kind of music. Of course, my parents won't let me listen to the hard stuff. That doesn't bother me much, though. There's so much cool Christian music and other neat pieces, I don't care about rock and rap." Just as his glance met Skye's, his dimples captured her heart.

Chad, you are so sweet, she couldn't help thinking. *And you're so wise.*

Melissa swept her fingers through her long blond curls. She grabbed a cloth from her case, removed her mouthpiece, and wiped out the barrel of the clarinet. "Some Christian kids get all bent out of shape 'cause they can't listen to their favorite music. Well, duh! Some of that stuff is just plain gross. The words are, like, creepy! What are we gonna do next, Mrs. C.? And by the way, where's your new foster kid—isn't her name Tanya something?"

Skye glanced from Chad to Melissa. "It's Tanya Bell and she's from Philly. She's in her room."

"How come?"

"She says she's a loner, and she hates just about everything but books."

"Give her a little space, kids," Mrs. Chambers said. "It's going to take awhile for her to get settled here. Robin, I'm very anxious for you to meet her. Maybe you can become friends, since you're so outgoing. After practice, we'll see if we can get her out here to meet all of you."

"Well, I did—sort of—meet her," Robin said with a disgusted look.

"Maybe this time the queen will let you into her court," Skye said, snickering.

"What was that?" Mrs. Chambers asked.

"Oh, nothing, Mom," Skye answered. Pushing her long hair back from her face, she shot a glance at Chad, who was still playing with his guitar strings. She then looked at Mrs. Chambers. "Hey, Mom, can we try 'Shine, Jesus, Shine'? Last week it almost sounded like a piece of music."

"Yeah," Bobby said. "Move over, Bach. It's time to do our thing! I bet if Bach ever heard us in concert, he'd turn over in his grave."

The room burst with laughter.

"Bobby, you are so ridiculous!" Morgan laughed.

"Where would we be without him?" Robin giggled.

Mrs. Chambers smoothed the pages in her music book. "Okay, kids, dig out that praise tune. Oh, I forgot to tell you—Skye's violin teacher, Mr. Baker, has been working on a special upbeat arrangement of 'Lord, Send Me Anywhere.' Do you think if we get started next week we can be ready to play that for the missions conference in April?"

"No way!" Morgan said, grinning.

"For real?" Skye beamed.

"You kids aren't as bad as you think," Mrs. Chambers said, facing the group. "All it'll take is a little extra practice. Are you game?"

"Sure." Chad's dimples flashed.

Robin flipped her pigtails back. "I'll just do a double practice on rainy days when the softball team is grounded. This sounds totally cool."

"There's nothing that would make Pop happier than me campin' out in the basement with my trumpet," Bobby said. "That way the walls downstairs will go out of their mind. But he won't."

Everyone laughed again.

By now, Mrs. Chambers' blue eyes were sparkling. "Well, this is great. If you want to go for it, I'll tell Pastor Newman to put you in the program for the conference. Of course, now you need an official name. So how shall we introduce this infamous group to the world?"

"Well, we're all part of the Youth for Truth church group," Melissa said. "Can't we use that somehow?"

"Hey, I got it!" Skye said. "Mom used the word 'ensemble' before. Why don't we just say the Youth for Truth Ensemble?"

"Yeah, I like that," Chad said. "That sounds very professional."

Everyone agreed.

"The Youth for Truth Ensemble it is," Mrs. Chambers said before turning back to the keyboard. "Okay, everyone, ready with this next piece? I'll use the harpsichord setting. We'll take it real slow the first time. I mean, really, really slow. We'll do double time when you know your parts better."

They all prepped their instruments.

"And I'm not goin' flat at the end this time," Skye declared, carefully positioning her bow.

Mrs. Chambers counted, "Then on four ... one and two and three and four ..." and the group played their hearts out.

Snyder County's ears never had it so good, Skye mused, sliding her bow gracefully across the strings. She smiled, pretending she and Chad were on center stage at Carnegie with thousands of people cheering them on. She turned to her last page, her foot keeping 4/4 time with the rest of the group. Carefully, she slid into the last chord and held it for the eight slowing beats.

"Hey, I did it!" she said. "I didn't flat on the ending!"

"Way to go, Skye," Chad yelled.

Mrs. Chambers smiled at the group. "You're getting it, gang. Morgan and Robin, you're both doing better on those triplets. Now, that's the way!" Her eyes darted to the arched entrance into the living room. "Well, hi, Tanya. How long have you been standing there?"

Everyone looked at Tanya.

Tanya crossed her arms and leaned up against the archway. "I just came in. I've been listening in my bedroom—I couldn't help it. The walls were dancing! But I've never heard such cool music. What was that you just played? And the one before it?"

Melissa rose from her chair next to Morgan. "That was a praise chorus we're learning for our missions conference."

Skye slid onto the sofa next to Chad and then looked at Tanya. "And the other one was 'Jesu, Joy of Man's Desiring' by Bach. My music teacher arranged these with more of an upbeat. Aren't they cool?"

"You mean that was classical and religious music?" Tanya's mouth fell open. "I thought all that stuff was for elevators and funerals. Of course, I've never really listened to it."

Mrs. Chambers pivoted toward Tanya. "Why don't you join us? I'd like you to meet everyone." She pointed, starting at her left. "Bobby Noll on trumpet, Chad Dressler on guitar, and you know Skye plays the violin. Melissa Richards plays the clarinet, and Morgan and Robin Ward each play flute. They're all better known as the world-famous Youth for Truth Ensemble. They start their tour of Europe next week."

Giggles intermingled with a barrage of hellos. "Yeah, right," Skye joked. "Not in this lifetime."

"Do you play an instrument, Tanya?" Melissa asked.

"Yeah," Bobby added. "We could always use a tuba."

The room exploded in laughter.

"He's just kidding," Morgan said. "But, for real, do you play one?"

Tanya shifted her weight and leaned against the wall again. "Nah. When I was little, Mother wanted me to take piano lessons, but I just wanted to listen to music, not play it. I guess if I had to choose, I'd rather just sing."

"Well, it's never too late to learn," Mrs. Chambers said. "Why don't you come over here and sit next to me while we finish practicing. If you'd like, just sing along. Most of these pieces have words to them."

"Nah—I'm not into that kind of stuff," Tanya said.

"Ah, c'mon. It's awesome," Skye said. *Maybe this will get her out of her bedroom.*

"Hey," Bobby added, "for now you can clap to the beat. We need some percussion anyway."

Everyone laughed. Tanya gave a half-smile. "Well ..."

Mrs. Chambers stood. "Please, Tanya. Sit here on the right side of the bench, and you can watch everything I do. I can always use a page turner."

"Yeah. C'mon," everyone chorused.

"Oh, all right," Tanya huffed. "Just this once."

chapter six

F or the umpteenth time, school is school!" Tanya snapped when Skye asked her how she was doing with new classes at Madison.

The three girls sat in the Chambers' game room late one Saturday morning, all lined up at the computers along the wall. Brilliant sunlight beamed through two high windows on the wall while the wooden entrance door rattled from the sharp February wind outside.

Skye wrestled with a controller, attacking "Superfly," her favorite motorcycle game. "Hey, are you two gonna make the honor roll? I've been workin' my head off to get a B in history. Then I'll make it."

Morgan had her eyes glued to the screen while she played Battleship online. "Zowie! Down goes your destroyer. You're sunk, Margie44, whoever you are." She glanced briefly at Skye and Tanya—then looked back at the game. "I have one minor problem before I get on the honor roll. It depends on what Mrs. Price gives me on my speech this Thursday. If I get a B in English, I'll make it."

Tanya relaxed in her chair, calmly moving her mouse button as she read something on the screen. "Well, if you two have to know, I've got straight A's right now. School's no problem for me. Studying for tests is a piece of cake. Hey, you should see the neat stuff I found out on the Web about mares and foals. There's tons of stuff here about how to care for them."

Skye put her whole body into working the controller. "Get back on the road, you idiot!" she yelled at the screen. Somehow, although engrossed in her game, she picked up Tanya's words. "Mom and Dad have all kinds of books upstairs about breeding. They've been into horses for years. Just ask them what you want to know."

"I'd rather find out myself," Tanya said smugly. "But I will ask to borrow their books. And the next time we go to the mall, I'm going to buy out the horse section of the bookstore. I have to help Belle and her baby make it through this. I just have to."

"What's with you and this horse?" Morgan said, never glancing away from the screen. "It's like you're big time obsessed with her or something. When you first came, you said you hated horses, and now all of a sudden, Belle can't burp without you goin' crazy."

Tanya looked at Morgan. "Horses burp?"

"She's just kidding!" Skye said. "You'd better do lots of reading about horses. You need it." Skye's game came to a musical end, and she started another round. "Hey, Tanya, have you tried to call your Aunt Barb yet?"

"Nah, maybe tomorrow," Tanya said, eyes returning to the screen. "Oh, this stuff is really cool. It shows a foal being born and everything. It tells exactly what to do to help the mare. I'm going to print this out so I have it when the time comes."

Skye spoke with a scolding tone. "Didn't Mom say at supper last night that you were definitely supposed to call your aunt today?"

"Hey, get this, Skye, and get it good. I'll call her when I'm good and ready."

"Tanya, you're gonna get it big time from Mom when she finds out. We're trying to help you."

"Don't say we didn't warn you," Morgan added. "And don't play little Miss Innocence when Mrs. C. faces you on her terms."

"Yeah, and this would be a bad time to get yourself grounded," Skye said. "Your parents are coming to see you next Saturday, aren't they? How would you explain that to them?"

"Will you two just cut it out?" Tanya's tone was sharp. "I wouldn't have to explain anything because they'd both know it wasn't be my fault. Nothing is ever my fault. So there!"

"And another thing," Skye insisted, "don't get all out of sorts over Belle's new baby. Doc Gonzalez—and Mom and Dad—will be here when it's born. They'll give Belle the best of care."

Morgan took her hand off the mouse, relaxed back into her wheelchair, and then giggled. "Four games of Battleship is enough for me. I feel a little seasick. Maybe I'll play a few games of Scrabble, just to get my brain out of water limbo."

"Hey, down there!" Mrs. Chambers yelled from the top of the stairs. "Lunch is ready. After we eat, Tanya, we can have a voice lesson for a while, if you'd like!"

"Be right there!" Skye answered.

Mrs. Chambers yelled again, "Morgan, do you want Mr. C. to help you with the chair lift, or do you want to go outside and come up the ramp?"

"I'll come up outside, Mrs. C.," Morgan said. "There's no ice or snow out there now, so I won't slide to Antarctica."

"Okay," Mrs. C. said. "I'll put the casserole out."

"Casserole. Not again!" Tanya complained. "Whatever happened to steak and baked potatoes?"

"Unreal," Skye said, gently placing her hand on Tanya's shoulder. "Keystone Stables' budget doesn't allow steak three times a week like you're used to."

Tanya pulled away. "Well, even once a week would be a break from the other trash I have to eat!"

After lunch, Mrs. Chambers and Tanya headed to the living room for Tanya's first voice lesson. Mr. Chambers went downstairs to his computer store/office in the basement, and Skye and Morgan got busy clearing off the table.

"Hey, Mom," Skye yelled, "can we sit in there and read while you two do your music thing? You know, 'girl' time?"

"That's up to Tanya," Mrs. Chambers answered. "Some kids get nervous when other people listen to them practice."

"That won't bother me in the least," Tanya yelled from the living room. "If they want to jeopardize their hearing, that's entirely up to them."

Mrs. Chambers added, "I certainly hope you girls weren't planning to do homework. It won't be very quiet."

Morgan turned the dishwasher on and headed toward the living room. "Nah, my homework's done. I'm reading this really neat book about the first seeing eye dog."

The wheelchair led the parade with Skye, Tippy, and Tyler following. Morgan parked by an end table, and Skye flopped on the sofa. The dogs found comfortable spots on the floor.

"Yeah, my homework won't take long," Skye said. "All I have to do is finish a report on Afghanistan. I'll do that later in my room. I'm reading this really cool story about a deaf boy who gets lost in the wilderness."

"Okay," Mrs. Chambers said. "Then all I ask of you two is no talking. Tanya needs to concentrate."

"No problem," Skye said, opening her book.

"My lips are zipped." Morgan giggled and then pulled her hand across her mouth.

Mrs. Chambers sat on the right side of the bench with Tanya sitting next to her. "Now let's pray and ask the Lord to help you do your best. Then we'll review your first scales."

Mrs. Chambers said a short prayer, and then Skye and Morgan started reading. Skye's mind drifted in and out of her book while catching all the action at the piano. *Tanya, you can be so cool when you want to be*, she thought.

Mrs. Chambers switched on the digital piano. "Now remember, Tanya, singing or playing any instrument is a gift from God. I'm so glad you're willing to try. Just have patience with yourself. You won't master it overnight. I've been playing the piano for years."

"Can I try singing that neat song you all were playing the other night?" Tanya asked. "I think it was 'Shine, Jesus, Shine.'"

"That will all come soon enough," Mrs. Chambers said. "For now you need to learn how to handle your voice and how to hit certain notes in beginner's scales. Once we figure out your range, then we can start with some simple praise tunes. Now, let's see you sit nice and straight and use your diaphragm to breathe. Okay, let's try the C scale."

Just as Tanya began, Skye's and Morgan's eyes met. Both girls smiled, and Skye gave a thumbs-up sign.

"Very good," Mrs. Chambers said to Tanya. "Now try your G scale slowly. You might not know this, young lady, but God has given you a beautiful voice. And you're picking up these scales beautifully."

"This is surprising me too," Tanya said. "I just never sang much. There was nothing to sing about." She went up and down her G scale.

"Good, Tanya," Mrs. Chambers said. "Now try it three more times. And don't tense up. That strains your voice, and you'll screech like a barn owl. Take it easy," Mrs. Chambers said lightly. "Enjoy yourself. This is supposed to be fun."

"Okay," Tanya said, repeating the scale. "That's cool," she said when she was finished.

"Tanya, I'd like to hear you sing something simple out of my book. I suppose since you've never gone to church much, you don't know any hymns or praise tunes, do you?" Mrs. Chambers asked.

"Not really," Tanya said. "But I really liked that one the group did during their practice. One thing I am good at is remembering how something sounds. Can we try that one?"

"Yeah, Mom," Skye interjected. "Let her try 'Shine, Jesus, Shine.' I know you have the words there."

"We can help by singing along—that is, if Tanya needs a backup group," Morgan said, giggling.

Mrs. Chambers turned sharply toward Skye "You are supposed to be reading, young lady." Then she looked at Morgan and smiled. "You too!"

"Oops, sorry," Morgan said and then lightly slapped her hand across her mouth.

"Sorry," Skye added.

Mrs. Chambers turned to the piano, then back toward the girls. "Aw, that's all right, girls. If Tanya doesn't mind, you two can join in. With her beautiful soprano voice, maybe we can work up some kind of trio for the missions conference as well. What do you say, Tanya?"

"Cool," Tanya said, "even though it will be in church."

Skye flopped her book on the sofa and stood behind Tanya. While Mrs. Chambers flipped through her chorus book, Morgan parked to the right of the bench.

"Let's see, 'Shine, Jesus, Shine.' Here it is, girls, and it's written in three-part harmony," Mrs. Chambers said.

"With the range of your voices, this should work out very nicely. Now, Tanya, you just sing the melody."

"Okay," Tanya said. "This is so cool."

Skye nudged Morgan in the shoulder, giving her another thumbs-up sign and a big, wide smile.

chapter seven

At noon the next Saturday, at a steakhouse near the mall, Mr. and Mrs. Chambers and Skye sat with Tanya and her parents.

Mr. Chambers wiped his mustache with a napkin. "It was very nice of you to invite us all to lunch, Dr. and Mr. Bell."

"Please call me Roger," the man across the table answered. "Chloris and I are more than glad to treat you before we visit Keystone Stables." He took a sip of water.

Munching on a hamburger and fries, Skye studied the husky man with broad shoulders. His tight curly hair was short and boring, she decided, and there was too much gray above his ears. But his dark eyes were awesome. His soft, deep voice sounded like the Christian disc jockey who played relaxing music at three o'clock in the morning. *Cool*, Skye thought. *Too cool.*

Dr. Bell's ruby red lips graced a cup of coffee. "Where's Morgan?"

"Oh, she had an emergency yearbook meeting at school," Skye said. "She wanted me to tell you that she was sorry she couldn't make it, but she'd probably see you at Keystone later this afternoon."

Tanya sat between her parents, zeroing in on her food. At last, she was enjoying her steak and baked potato.

Mrs. Chambers finished a bite of her salad, then her eyes focused on Mr. Bell. "Roger, I understand that you are away from home quite a lot."

Mr. Bell casually rubbed the back of his neck. "Yes, as much as I hate it, it's my job."

"What exactly is your line of work?" Mr. Chambers asked.

"I own a building supply company in South Philly," Mr. Bell answered. "We supply contractors who do large projects like skyscrapers and factory shells. Unfortunately, I have to spend a lot of time on the road or in the air making contacts with clients. I just returned from California."

"He's never home," Tanya mumbled through a mouthful of food. "Neither is Mother."

Dr. Bell played with her baked potato. "Tanya, we've been over this a thousand times."

"Now, Baby," Mr. Bell said, "you know we can't help it. We have to work so you can have nice things."

"But do you have to work all the time?" Tanya growled.

Skye's glance darted around the table like she was watching a tennis match.

Mr. Chambers changed the subject. "Well, even though Tanya's been with us only a few weeks, I think you'll both be pleased with her progress." He turned to Skye. "You're such good friends. Don't you think this is accurate?"

"Yeah," Skye agreed, "she's not hibernating in her room anymore since she got interested in Southern Belle and started singing."

"Southern Belle?" Mr. Bell asked. "Is that a TV program?"

"Singing?" Dr. Bell asked.

"Southern Belle's a horse, Father," Tanya declared.

"A horse?" Tanya's parents raised their voices in unison.

"Yes, a horse," Tanya said.

"Since when do you like horses—or any animals for that matter?" Dr. Bell looked squarely at her daughter. "And what's this about singing?"

"Yes, tell us," Mr. Bell said, reaching over and patting Tanya's hand.

Tanya grabbed her glass of soda as though her father's hand had never touched her.

"This is a new you," he said with enthusiasm. "Have you learned to ride too?"

Tanya sipped her drink. "I will in the spring when the ice and snow are gone."

Mrs. Chambers worked the knife and fork on her steak. "Tanya's really interested in caring for the horse because Southern Belle is going to foal in the spring. When Tanya's not doing homework, she's down at the barn. Oh, speaking of school, tell your parents how it's going."

"Straight A's," Tanya said between bites of potato.

"That's the way," Mr. Bell said. "Chloris, I told you she'd keep those grades up in her new school. You did all that worrying for nothing."

Dr. Bell sipped more coffee and sampled her salad. "Have you made any friends?" she asked.

"Nah, not really. They're not my style," Tanya spouted off.

I guess that includes me, Skye surmised. "Hey, Tanya, what about the kids in our Youth for Truth group—and the music ensemble?" Skye gave Tanya a quick smile.

"Oh, yeah," Tanya said like she had deliberately forgotten. "They're all right, I guess."

Mr. Chambers smiled. "Tanya, please tell your mother about your singing lessons before she has a cardiac right here in the restaurant."

"You're taking singing lessons?" Dr. Bell asked, surprise written all over her face.

Tanya cut another piece of steak and took her time chewing it.

Mrs. Chambers' words flowed out of her as she looked at Tanya. "This is the biggest surprise of all. This young lady has a wonderful gift from God. Tanya, go on. Tell them."

Tanya finished chewing and then guzzled a big drink of soda. "Oh, all right," she finally said, "but I still don't see what the big deal is. Mrs. Chambers says I have a really nice voice and that I should keep taking lessons."

"Well, that's super, Baby!" Mr. Bell said. "We've been wanting you to have an interest in something other than reading—not that there's anything wrong with reading. But ... we ... are you going to sing something for us later?"

Dr. Bell agreed. "That is very good news." She shot her glance from Tanya to Mrs. Chambers. "She's learned to sing in just a few weeks?"

Mrs. Chambers wiped her mouth with the napkin and placed it back on her lap. "Your daughter has a natural God-given talent, Dr. Bell. With the proper training, she could develop a beautiful style."

The Bells hung on every word. Tanya chewed delicately and quietly, finishing her baked potato and washing it down with a glass of soda.

Mr. Bell emptied his glass of water. "That's great," he said. "If you really like singing, when you come home you may take all the singing lessons you want. Would you like that?"

Tanya shrugged, never looking at her father.

Tanya, when will you ever appreciate what you have?
Skye wondered.

"Miss," Dr. Bell said, flagging down a passing waitress. "More coffee, please." She turned back to the table. "Neither Roger nor I have any musical interests except to play CDs and the radio. It would be quite interesting to find out if anyone else in Tanya's family is musically inclined. Mrs. Chambers, you say she has a—how did you put it—a God-given talent?"

"Absolutely!" Mrs. Chambers said.

The waitress brought a pot of coffee and refilled Dr. Bell's cup. "Anyone else?" she asked.

All declined.

"Thank you," Dr. Bell said, refocusing on the discussion. "After we're finished at Keystone Stables, we plan to visit Tanya's aunt Barb. Tanya can ask her about any singing talent in the family."

Tanya just shrugged.

Dr. Bell continued, "Well, when we get back to Philly, I'll call Tanya's grandmother. If anyone knows anything about that family, it would be her."

"Father," Tanya said, perking up in her chair and flashing her eyes at her dad, "can we go to the bookstore before you leave?"

"Sure. What do you need?"

"I'm looking for books about horses, especially pregnant ones."

"Maybe your mother could help you. That is her line of work," he answered.

"Not really." Dr. Bell chuckled. "I might have worked on some old gray mares and young fillies, if you know what I mean, but never on a real horse."

Everyone joined in the laughter except Tanya.

Mr. Bell's laughter reminded Skye of the Santa at the mall in December. *Double cool*, she thought.

"Baby," Mr. Bell said between chuckles, "your new interest in horses makes me very happy. This might be a good time to discuss an important decision your mother and I have made."

Tanya sighed. "What now?" she complained.

"First of all," Mr. Bell started, "we've been thinking about this for an awfully long time, but we never mentioned it to you because you didn't seem to like animals. We thought you'd absolutely hate the idea."

They're buying Tanya her own zoo, Skye figured.

Dr. Bell sipped her coffee. "Tanya, your father and I are thinking of moving."

"Where?" Tanya asked through a half yawn as though her mother had just asked her to pick up a pencil off the floor.

Mr. and Mrs. Chambers were studying the interaction going on across the table. Mr. Chambers folded his arms, and Mrs. Chambers leaned on the table and took a slow sip of water.

"Now don't get upset," Mr. Bell said. "You can still go to Ridgecrest—if that's what you're worried about. You'll still have all of your friends."

What friends? Skye thought, scratching her head.

"I'm not upset," Tanya informed her parents without the slightest hint of irritation. "But where?"

Dr. Bell said, "Your father wants to buy a farm in north Jersey."

"A what?" Tanya peaked her eyebrows.

"Now think about this," Mr. Bell said. "We've all talked about how crazy city life is. I'm at the place in my business where I can start mandating responsibilities to our field representatives. I'd like to spend more time with you and your mother. At the first of the year, I'm planning to begin part-time as a consultant." He looked at Mr. and Mrs. Chambers. "I grew up on a farm and loved working the soil and breathing fresh air." He looked back at his daughter and touched her hand again. "If you want a horse, you can have any kind you'd like."

This time Tanya's hand stayed put. She stared out the window, deep in thought. "Hmm," is all she said.

Dr. Bell released a beautiful smile as she grasped Tanya's other hand. "Well, that's one more word than I expected to hear. I think we can take that as a yes."

"Tanya," Skye added, "this is great. Think of all the things you're learning at Keystone that will help you on your own farm, especially with horses."

"Any kind of horse I want?" Tanya asked, still staring.

"Any kind at all," Mr. Bell answered.

chapter eight

The month of March in Pennsylvania brought the promise of an early spring. Although the threat of snow had been predicted over the next week, crocuses were already poking their colorful heads out of Mrs. Chambers' softening flowerbeds.

With the excitement of warmer weather on its way, family discussions centered around the horses. Skye and Morgan were already planning what events they would enter at the Snyder County Horse Show in August.

Mr. and Mrs. Chambers and Tanya focused on Belle and her foal. Tanya continued to surprise everyone, not only with her willingness to sing but also with the huge amount of time she devoted to Southern Belle.

However, as hard as Skye and Morgan tried to be friends, Tanya brushed them off like dandruff. Most of her free time was spent in the barn or hidden away in her bedroom, singing along with Christian CDs or reading her hundreds of books. She came to the table for meals when called, but then lately she'd been griping her way through her chores. A hundred times Skye had made up her mind to ignore Tanya, but it was hard, she found out, to ignore someone living right under her nose. Frustrated beyond words, Skye longed for Saturday when she and Mrs. Chambers would have some time alone.

"Well, Skye, how did this week go in school?" Mrs. Chambers said as the two rode their horses the following Saturday on a trail through the back woods. The Westies romped close by.

Skye reached down and patted Champ's fuzzy neck. "Pretty good, Mom. I think I'll make the honor roll again if I can just remember where Persia was on an ancient history map. Oh, and I've been wanting to ask you if it would be all right if I could be the manager of the girls' softball team. Robin's been after me forever to join the team. But you know sports and I get along like scrambled eggs and pickles. Being the manager is the best I can do for Robin. Filling a water cooler and carrying a first aid kit shouldn't be that hard."

"First, let's consider how busy you are throughout the week," Mrs. Chambers said. "Find out how many days you need to stay after school for the team. Since you only have Maranatha counseling once a week, perhaps you can squeeze softball in somewhere. Are you sure you can fit that in with all your studies, music lessons, and barn chores?"

"No problem," Skye assured her. "Mom, I need to ask you something," she said, suddenly changing the subject.

"Yes, honey, what is it?"

Skye chose her next words carefully while the horses' bridles clanked and the saddles squeaked. The group headed out of the woods and across a field to a gentle hill a short distance behind the Chambers' barn. Nudging Champ to trot alongside Pepsi, Skye finally mustered enough courage to speak.

"Mom, what can I do about . . ." Skye hesitated.

"About what?"

"About ..."

"About Tanya?" Mrs. Chambers asked.

"Hey!" Skye said. "You knew all along."

"It's pretty obvious that you're having trouble liking her. What seems to be the problem?"

"What's the problem?" Skye squawked. "How's this for starters? I have tried and tried to be nice to her, but most of the time, she acts like I'm not even there. I wish she'd go home." Her face flushed hot from embarrassment the instant she realized what she had just said. "Sorry, but that's the way I feel."

With the dogs trailing behind, the horses made their way to the top of the hill. The view opened up into a panorama of farmers' fields. In the distance, the gray bulges of Shade Mountain melded into a steel-blue sky layered with fast-moving clouds. A March wind teased Skye's long hair that flowed out from under her hardhat. She pushed her hair back and pulled her jacket zipper up tight against her neck.

Mrs. Chambers stroked Pepsi's neck, and then rested an arm across the horn of the saddle. She focused on the view, the wind playing with her tied-down Stetson. "It's awfully difficult living with someone you don't like. Honey, let me ask you a few questions. Let's see if we can get to the root of this problem."

"It's not that I don't like her. But she is a problem!" Skye shot off.

Mrs. Chambers gave Skye her familiar careful-young-lady look. "Skye ..."

"Oh, all right. Go ahead, shoot."

"Exactly when did you decide that you didn't like Tanya? It is a decision, you know. It doesn't just happen by itself."

Skye stared at the valley, thinking into the past. "Like, when she threw Morgan and me out of her bedroom right after she got here. She just thinks she's better than everybody else. She acts like some kind of queen bee or something. That's all."

"Are you sure? Think carefully."

Out of the distant past, Skye's memory taunted her.

"Skye, are you with me?" Mrs. Chambers asked.

"Yes-s-s," Skye squeezed out. "Okay, okay. I guess I didn't like her from the first time I met her—when she was with Kenny Hartzell at the fair. She made fun of me and called me a farmer. It was her fault I drank that beer." Her voice rose in anger.

"Now listen to yourself, Skye. What are you doing? That old problem you've had long before you moved in seems to have resurfaced."

Skye felt her face redden again, and her insides started to sizzle with anger—an anger she thought she had buried with her past. Tears of shame welled up in her eyes. "I'm blaming someone else for what I did wrong," she lamented.

"I think you're correct on that one," Mrs. Chambers said. "Remember, Skye, God holds us responsible for our actions. Thankfully, you have asked the Lord to forgive you. But every once in a while, our bad habits poke their heads out just like the ugly weeds trying to choke my crocuses. Here's another question, and this one's loaded. Are you ready?"

"Shoot."

"Are you jealous of Tanya?"

Skye recoiled as though Tanya had asked her the question herself.

"Skye?"

"Jealous? Of her?" Skye tsked. "Of course not! Why should I be?"

"Are you jealous of her time with me?"

"Nah, I know that's your job."

"Well, let's see. She has two parents ..."

61

"But I have you and Dad."

"And she has everything she wants—and then some."

"She's spoiled rotten."

"Well?"

"Well, what?"

"Do you wish you had some of that money? Some of her stuff?"

"Well—maybe," Skye conceded. "But I don't hate her for that. She's—she's—just so—immature! Nobody likes her at school either! Just ask Morgan!"

Mrs. Chambers turned Pepsi around and faced Skye, eyeball to eyeball. "Honey, Tanya has some deep-rooted problems that haven't even surfaced. That's why she's here at Keystone Stables and Maranatha. Can't you remember how it was when you first moved in? You were all torn up inside. You were so full of bitterness against your parents that you couldn't see straight."

"Yeah, I was a mess, wasn't I?" Skye agreed. "I just never think of Tanya having problems. Why would she have problems? She has everything else."

"Yes, Tanya, does have everything as far as material things, but she's a very lonely young lady," Mrs. Chambers said. "She's chosen to isolate herself from everyone because she hurts so deeply inside. Let me tell you something, Skye. When someone like Tanya acts like she's better than everybody, it's usually because she has a low opinion of herself. There's something bothering her that she's not willing to share with us yet. She needs a lot of love and understanding from all of us. Now, let me ask you a very serious question."

"Okay."

"Have you prayed for Tanya—even once?"

Silence.

Mrs. Chambers pointed upward. "Skye, you know that when you accepted Christ, your life really started to change for the better. He helped you get over your bitterness and gave you a wonderful peace in your heart. Tanya's empty inside and she's scared. I could be wrong, but I'm afraid she doesn't know the Lord."

"I never thought of her being scared of anything but horses, but that was only when she first moved in."

"One last question, and then we'll head back." Mrs. Chambers gave Skye a warm smile. "Will you promise to pray for her from now on? Just remember, honey, she is right where you once were."

Skye had focused on her saddle, but the warmth in Mrs. Chambers' voice drew her back to her mom's caring smile. *Mom really does love me*, she thought. *She loves all of us.* "Yeah, I promise to pray for Tanya," Skye finally said. "Every day."

chapter nine

The entire family had lined up at the cross ties in the barn watching Dr. Gonzales examine Southern Belle. Mr. Chambers was holding the mare steady. Afternoon rays from the warm spring sun filtered in through the doorway of the barn.

"She's coming early." Dr. Gonzales sighed as he finished. He wiped his hands on a cloth and placed the stethoscope and other equipment back in his big black bags. "I sure was hoping for next month, but she'll be an April baby."

"She?" asked Skye.

"Yep," the doctor answered. "You've got yourself a little filly in there. Mighty, mighty little."

"What does that mean?" Tanya's voice conveyed raw panic.

"That's not a good sign, is it, Doc?" Mr. Chambers said.

"I'm afraid not," the doctor answered. "Belle seems stronger, but we can't be sure of her either. We needed that extra month for both of them to put on more weight with good food and vitamins. It's gonna be a close call."

"What can we do to help?" Morgan asked.

Mrs. Chambers stepped up to Belle, kissed her on the nose, and stroked her neck. "From this point on, she needs around-the-clock care, doesn't she, Doc? We had another mare like this a few years ago, and we pulled both of them through with tons of TLC."

"We have to save them! We just have to!" Tanya exploded. Crying hysterically, she ran out of the barn.

Skye gave Mrs. Chambers a "what now?" look.

"Go after her, Skye," Mrs. Chambers said. "I'll be there as soon as we're done here with the doc."

Outside Skye found Tanya hunched over the paddock fence next to the barn. Face buried in her arms, she was wailing like Belle and the baby had just died.

"Tanya, what's with you?" Skye said roughly before she remembered Mrs. Chambers' words. *Love and understanding.* Slowly Skye placed her hand on the weeping girl's shoulder. Tanya did not pull away.

"I love that horse," Tanya wailed. She turned slowly, her face drenched with free-flowing tears.

What can I possibly say to make her feel better? Skye pondered. *"She is where you once were, honey,"* she remembered Mrs. Chambers saying.

"We all love her," Skye said softly. "We'll help her pull through."

Tanya wiped her eyes with the back of her hands. "Didn't Mrs. Chambers say that Belle needed care all the time, like, through the night too? What did she mean?"

"It's not that she needs care twenty-four/seven. It's just that Belle and the baby have a much better chance if the vet or even Dad is right there when the foal comes. She's gonna need help delivering. If the foal decides to be born during the night when no one is with Belle, it could be a bad scene. We just need to keep watch all the time. That's what she meant."

Just as Skye finished speaking, Mrs. Chambers rushed out of the barn. "Tanya, are you all right?"

"Aw, she's just upset because of Belle," Skye said.

Tanya took one step forward, her eyes pleading for a mother's embrace. But she stopped. "Mrs. C., I want to move into the barn and take care of Belle. Please! I just have to do this."

From a horse hater to a horse lover in one easy lesson! Skye mused. Go figure!

"Well, I'll talk with Tom about it. But, Tanya, are you sure you want to do this? It can get mighty lonesome in the barn with no one around but four-legged friends."

They'll be better company than the stupid bears in her bedroom, Skye thought.

"I won't mind." Tanya managed a stingy smile through her sniffles. "I want to do this. P-l-e-a-s-e!"

I really don't hate her at all, Skye told herself. I just feel sorry for her. And she is trying to help. "There's a cot in the tack room," she offered. "We can help bring down a heavy sleeping bag and some of your things. And we can tell you what signs to look for when the baby's coming."

"Let's do it right now." Tanya's eyes sparkled through her pain.

Mrs. Chambers added her concerns. "Now, you'll need to come to the house for your meals, family devotions, and your voice lessons."

"And your showers!" Skye said.

"Will someone watch Belle while I do that?" Tanya rambled on, fear sweeping over her face. "And school? And Maranatha? Who'll watch her when I'm away? Can't I just stay with her all the time?"

Mrs. Chambers reached out and touched Tanya's shoulder. "Don't worry, Tanya! Tom will be here all day, every day. Even when he's doing other things, he'll check on her every hour or so. She'll be all right."

"But I still want to do this! Thank you, Mrs. C.," Tanya added.

"Okay," Mrs. Chambers said. "Let's go talk with Tom and see what he says."

Tanya's face beamed. "This is too perfect," she said. "I have a report due on Monday about my strangest experience. Sleeping in a barn! Too cool!"

And I could write a book! Skye concluded, and broke into a smile as the three headed back into the barn.

"It's a breech. The rump's coming out first," Dr. Gonzales lamented. "I was afraid she wouldn't turn in time." He had positioned himself behind Belle in the far corner of her box stall on a soft bed of hay. Belle lay stretched out on her side, moaning. The vet's hands, protected in surgical gloves up to his elbows, reached toward the back of the horse. Mr. Chambers sat near the door of the stall and held Belle's head in his lap. Mrs. Chambers and the girls watched from outside the stall through the wire mesh and open doorway. Sunrise was still three hours away.

"I'm sure glad you folks called me when you did," Dr. Gonzales said. "This little girl is going to need all the help she can get—and then some. It's going to be rough."

Moaning, Belle kicked her back legs, trying to get up.

"Easy, girl," Mr. Chambers said, pressing his weight on Belle's neck. "You stay put. Let those contractions push your baby out."

"We have Tanya to thank for getting you here so soon," Mrs. Chambers said. "For the last three weeks, she's hardly let Belle out of her sight."

"And I knew an hour ago it had to be time, the way Belle was prancing and pawing and carrying on," Tanya said, massaging her hands. "Belle had every animal in the barn wide awake."

"Yeah," Skye added, "and when the phone rang in the middle of the night, we knew Tanya wasn't making a social call."

The chuckles were weak. Everyone was watching the mare struggle.

"C'mon, Belle, push!" Dr. Gonzales yelled, his hands locked on the foal's protruding rump. Under the shadow of his baseball cap, he turned bright red and sweat trickled down both sides of his face.

Belle's whole body twitched, and she let out a long, tortuous moan.

"She looks so helpless," Tanya practically screamed. "Can't we do anything?"

Mrs. Chambers slipped her arm around Tanya. "We can help by staying calm. She doesn't need to sense that we're all upset. That will only make things worse. We just have to let nature take its course."

"Yeah, and a little prayer would help right now," Morgan added.

For the next thirty minutes, Dr. Gonzales and Mr. Chambers did all they could to help Belle deliver her foal. Belle struggled with every contraction, giving life to her little foal, inch by inch, the doctor using all the strength he had to pull the baby free.

"We've got to get this filly's head out quick now," the doctor said as he grasped its shoulders and pulled slowly and firmly. "Come on, Belle, just one more push. Come on, baby."

"Easy girl," Mr. Chambers said, stroking Belle's lathered neck. "You can do it."

The mare gave one long push, eyes wild, body writhing in pain, then the doctor pulled the filly free. Belle turned her head back, looked at the foal and nickered, then placed her tired head back down on Mr. Chambers' lap.

"She's out!" Skye tried to contain her excitement as the doctor wiped the foal with soft, clean cloths. "Will you look at that! She's gorgeous!"

"What a beautiful cocoa color!" Mrs. Chambers said. "Four white socks—and look at her darling face! She has a star right on her forehead."

"Wow!" Tanya said. "I've never seen anything like this. She is too awesome!"

"Way to go, Belle," Morgan said from the doorway. "You should be proud. That's one fine baby!"

Dr. Gonzales continued to clean and stimulate the foal that lay in a little wet ball on the hay. "This little girl is all legs, and they're very weak. Tom, we need to get Belle up soon. The baby needs her first meal in about twenty minutes. We'll have to help both to stand."

Mr. Chambers carefully slipped out from under Belle's head and stood. He stared at her as she lay stretched out. "Doc, there's something wrong here. She's not breathing right."

Belle lay still, nothing moving but her belly that rose and fell with short, choppy breaths.

The doctor rushed to Belle's side, placing his stethoscope on the horse's chest. "This was a mighty rough delivery, Tom."

Tanya placed both hands over her mouth, stifling a scream she knew she couldn't release. Her eyes filled with tears. "What's wrong? Is she gonna make it? She has to!"

Skye glanced from Tanya to the mare. The vet stood and backed away. "She's lost a lot of blood, and there must be internal bleeding. We better not try to get her up."

Almost as though determined to prove him wrong, Belle started to move her legs. She struggled with every ounce of strength left in her to obey her instincts. She tried to stand—she wanted to—to welcome her baby into the world, to feed it, to love it. She labored to hold her head up, nostrils flaring wildly.

"Easy, girl," Mr. Chambers said, stepping forward and pressing against her neck. She struggled and kicked again and then slowly lay her head back down. She moaned horribly, her tired body letting out one last breath, and then she lay still with not even her belly moving.

"Aw, no," Mr. Chambers said, his eyes filling with tears. "I'm afraid we've lost her."

Dr. Gonzales scrambled to his knees, pressing the stethoscope to different parts of Belle's chest and sides. He stopped, and his shoulders slumped. He stood and relaxed his cap back further on his head. His eyes, too, filled with tears as he shook his head in disbelief. "She's—she's—gone," he struggled to say.

Mr. Chambers knelt down and gently stroked Belle's neck, tears trickling down the man's sad face. "She was just too weak," his voice wavered. "Hon, we're gonna need blankets and bottles for the baby. We don't want to lose her too."

"I've got formula in my truck," Dr. Gonzales said somberly.

Skye fought the unwanted tears that flooded her eyes and now ran freely down over her burning cheeks. She glanced at Morgan who sat staring in disbelief at the mare. Her freckled face flushed and instantly her eyes turned red and watery.

"We want to help ..." Skye started to say.

"No! This can't be!" Tanya screamed. "She can't be dead! She can't be!" The hysterical girl pushed her way into the stall and fell on the mare's silent belly, sobbing uncontrollably as she ran her fingers through the horse's chestnut coat. "You can't be dead! You can't be! It's my fault again!"

"Tanya, it's all right," Mr. Chambers said. He touched her shoulder and looked back at his wife. *Help me!* his watery eyes said.

Man, she's taking this hard, Skye thought, wiping her eyes. "Mom ..." she pleaded, looking into blue eyes already pouring out streams of tears.

Mrs. Chambers wiped her cheeks and took a deep breath. She rushed into the stall next to Tanya and touched her shoulders, urging her to stand. But Tanya pulled away, clinging to the horse like it was her own mother. "You can't die. I won't let you!" she wailed.

"Tom," Dr. Gonzales said, scooping up the filly in his arms. "Let's get this baby set up in one of your clean stalls. She needs rest—and quiet."

The men headed toward an empty stall on the other side of the barn. "Hon," Mr. Chambers said, "I'll be back as soon as I can. Morgan, come with us. You can start heating the formula for the baby."

Tears flowing down her face, Skye slipped into the stall and knelt next to Tanya. Mrs. Chambers knelt on Tanya's other side. All three sat weeping.

"Tanya," Skye finally cried softly, "this wasn't your fault. You took care of her as well as you possibly could. Sometimes things like this just happen."

Mrs. Chambers slipped her arm around Tanya and struggled to speak through a flood of tears. "Like Skye said, things like this just happen. Please don't forget about that baby. She needs a lot of care."

Slowly, Tanya raised her head. Her whole body quivered as she reached forward and gently stroked the dead horse's neck. "Belle," Tanya finally said, "nothing is ever going to happen to your baby. I'll see to that. She will live and grow strong. She'll be beautiful—just like you were. I promise!"

chapter ten

M r. Chambers closed his Bible, ending the family's evening devotions. It had been several days since they had lost Belle. "Remember, girls," he said, "First Corinthians chapter 13 is considered the Love Chapter of the Bible. When you are struggling with how to show love to each other, read that a few hundred times." His mustache twitched. "I think you'll get the idea."

Mrs. Chambers' blue eyes smiled. "Yes, it's easy to say 'I love you,' but putting your words into action is another matter. Now if you recall, last week we asked you girls to find a special way to show love at school this week. Would any of you like to share your experience?"

The room was silent.

"Don't worry, girls," Mr. Chambers joked. "This is not a test, just a sharing time."

"Oh, I know!" Morgan raised her hand. "This week in math — we're doing graphs and stuff — Pam Housenick didn't have a clue. She asked me to help her in study hall, and I'd already planned to use that period to finish a science report that was due the next day. Well, I said yes and helped her. I finished my report at home that night, which cost me big time. I had to sacrifice my hour of Battleship time."

"Would you say that was a great big sacrifice?" Mrs. Chambers raised her eyebrows.

"Nah, not really," Morgan said. "I felt good about helping Pam. She's a cool kid, but she just doesn't get the hang of math. I already told her I'd help her again. Maybe she won't flunk it this semester."

"Very nice," Mr. Chambers said. "Morgan, I think you've probably already discovered that the one who gives love benefits as much as the one receiving it."

"Yeah, that's cool," Morgan agreed.

"Anyone else?" Mrs. Chambers asked.

Skye's mind flashed back to one of her bus rides to school. "Monday morning—you know when everybody storms off the buses and charges to their lockers just to get the latest scoop of weekend news? Well, I couldn't wait to tell Robin and some of the other kids about our new filly—and poor Belle.

"I ran off the bus and was flying up the steps into the school when this pathetic little kid—I don't even know his name—tripped right in front of me. He went down hard, right on the cement. His backpack strap tore, and everything spilled out: books, pencils, candy bars, money, everything! It was a disaster. I started to go around him, and just that quick, I felt something—or someone—tell me to help him out. So I did. By the time I got to my locker, everybody else was gone, and it was just about time for the bell. I barely made it to my first class in time."

"And how did you feel, Skye?" Mr. Chambers asked.

"Pooped!" Skye said. "I was sweatin' up a storm. But then when I got settled in class, I really felt good that I had helped someone."

"That's the idea," Mrs. Chambers said. "Love in action." She looked at Tanya. "And, young lady, how about you?"

Tanya examined her newly-polished nails. "I really forgot about it," she said glibly, then glanced at her watch. "Can I go now? It's time for the baby's feeding."

"Dad, speaking of babies," Skye said, "aren't we gonna name this new little one? Or are we just gonna call her 'Baby' from now on?"

"No, we're going to name her," Mr. Chambers replied. "But Eileen and I've been searching the Internet for information about Belle's bloodlines. She has papers that indicate she was from a line of champion Quarter Horses. I don't know why she showed up at auction in such terrible condition. The filly does need a name—but it's got to be a good one. Hang on for a few more days. Hopefully, we'll find out more about the line that little girl comes from."

"No problem!" Skye said.

"Can I go now?" Tanya said, perturbed. "The baby really needs a bottle."

"Yes, Tanya," Mrs. Chambers said, "you may go."

Tanya jumped up from the sofa and headed out of the living room.

"Remember, Tanya, the bottle must be heated to the proper temperature," Mr. Chambers warned. "And make sure the barn door is closed tight. Drafts could make the foal sick. I'll be down in a little while to check her out."

"I know," Tanya said, grabbing her jacket from the hall closet.

Mrs. Chambers glanced Tanya's way. "Do you have your homework all finished?" she said loudly.

"Yeah. I got it all done in school. Later," Tanya yelled as she slammed the kitchen door.

"I can't figure her out!" Morgan said. "What is with her and that foal? She's obsessed. And I never saw anyone cry over an animal dying like she did with Belle. She only knew her a few months. It was like they were soul mates, or something."

Skye folded her arms and crossed her legs. "She sure was upset. I didn't know what to say, or do!"

"Girls, a lot of things are bothering Tanya," Mr. Chambers said and then glanced at his wife.

"That's right," Mrs. Chambers said. "You girls know that when you keep something hidden inside for so long, it's awfully hard to get it out. Tanya is making some progress in counseling, but she's still got a long way to go. Now, we just had a discussion about love. How have you two been showing love to Tanya—or doesn't she count?"

Skye stared at the floor.

"She doesn't give us a chance!" Morgan piped. "She's always busy."

"Yeah," Skye added. "We want to be nice to her, but she's always down at the barn."

"Well, girls," Mr. Chambers said, "God must work in Tanya's heart just like he did in yours. Until then we'll all keep praying and allowing God to love her through us. Sooner or later she'll come around. Just be patient."

"Let's think a minute," Mrs. Chambers said. "How could you show her love around here—even though she acts like she doesn't want it?"

"Send her a Valentine card every day!" Skye said sarcastically, looking around the room.

Everyone laughed.

Morgan twisted her mouth, placing her fingers on her chin. "Well, she doesn't need any help with homework. She's got straight A's, so that won't work. She probably could help me if she'd ever look beyond her own nose at other people's problems."

"Aw, come on now," Mrs. Chambers urged, "what could you two do to help her?"

Morgan raised her hand. "Hey, I know. I could cook her favorite meal once in a while. I love to cook. She loves to eat—certain things. That's what I'm gonna do."

"You can start with queen bee soup," Skye said and laughter filled the room.

"Skye ..." Mr. Chambers chided. "Let's hear your idea."

Skye stared at her sneakers. "Hmm," she finally said, looking up. "I guess I could offer to help her with the foal. Maybe I could heat the formula or help clean the stall. Yeah, that's what I'll do—starting right now."

Skye opened the Dutch door and slipped inside the foal's box stall located in the warmest corner of the barn. Tanya was kneeling with her arm around the baby's neck, feeding her from a large plastic bottle. The filly, standing on wobbly legs, was sucking the nipple like it was her last meal. A bright pink halter hugged her petite, fuzzy head. The stall almost sparkled from Tanya's obvious care. A thick layer of fresh straw covered a spotlessly clean floor. Fighting her negative feelings, Skye once again made up her mind to be kind. "Hey, how's it going?" she asked.

"Cool," Tanya said. "Look at her scarfing down the formula. She loves to eat. Isn't she awesome?"

"Yeah, she's something else. I just love her chocolate milk color," Skye said. She tiptoed closer and knelt beside the foal, touching her softly on her neck. "Do you know what else is too cool?"

"What?"

"Now I mean this as a compliment, not a jab. You two are almost the same color. That is super awesome."

Tanya held her hand next to the filly's face. "Hey, we are! Wow! That is too sweet!"

"Maybe we should call her 'Sweetie Pie,' " Skye said, giggling.

"I would love to name her," Tanya said, "but I know the Chambers are searching for just the right nomenclature."

"Nomenclature?"

"Just a fancy word for 'name,'" Tanya said with a grin. "What would you call her?"

"I haven't really thought about it that much because I figured I wouldn't have the chance to name her."

"Well, for sure, she's gonna need a name. She'll be a beauty the way you're taking care of her. And I'll help you anyway I can. Just ask," Skye said.

"Right on. I have a journal where I mark down every time I feed her, what she gets fed, and how much other stuff she gets. She hasn't missed a thing. Don't you think she looks bigger?"

"Sure," Skye said. "She's made a lot of headway in two weeks. Every day she'll get stronger. How do you like motherhood?"

"Motherhood? What do you mean?" Tanya's face grew serious.

"Well, she's gonna think you're her mother. She'll follow you around like a lost puppy."

"No kidding!" Tanya's eyes widened.

"I'm not kidding." Skye ran her hand down over the foal's fuzzy brown back. "Those big brown eyes see you as her mama. Congratulations, Mom!"

chapter eleven

A … gimme a B … Mrs. C.," Chad said, tuning his guitar in the Chambers' living room. "Then a D and an E next. Hey, get it? The 'ABCs' with Mrs. C."

Skye giggled at Chad while she tightened the strings on her violin. The kids in the Youth for Truth Ensemble also laughed and prepped their instruments.

Mrs. Chambers hit a B on the digital piano, then paged through her music book. "I guess we could warm up with a few of your favorites before we work on the 'Lord, Send Me Anywhere' medley. It's coming along fine. Do you all realize that the missions conference is next week already? And I, for one, am so thankful Tanya is singing two solos. Hearing the words to such beautiful songs will be an added blessing to the congregation."

"Where is she?" Melissa asked.

"In the barn," Morgan said. "She's taking care of our new foal. In fact, she's living down there with it."

"I've tried to call several times," Mrs. Chambers added, "but the heavy rain hitting the barn roof must have drowned out the phone."

"Mom, do you want me to go down for her?" Skye asked.

"I hate to send you out in this deluge, but since the man of the house is on a business call, I'd sure appreciate it. Are you sure you don't mind?"

"No problem," Skye said. "I'll be back in a sec."

"Do you want me to go?" Chad asked.

"Nah, that's okay," Skye said, standing and resting her violin on the sofa. She gazed into Chad's big brown eyes and her heart melted. *So sweet!*

"Put your hood up," Mrs. Chambers said. "And take Tanya's raincoat with you. She didn't have it when she went to the barn earlier. She should've taken it."

"Once a mother, always a mother," Bobby said. "My mother even made me wear boots tonight 'cause she heard it might rain!"

"Yeah," Robin added, "my mother will be telling me until I'm forty to cover my head in the rain."

Everyone chuckled.

Chad strummed his guitar like he had to finish his entire practice in five seconds. "Let's try 'The God of All Heavens.' It's been ages since we did that."

At the closet, Skye put on her raincoat, grabbed Tanya's, and slipped out the back door. She stepped off the porch, pulling her hood string tightly as the rain pelted off her head. She took a deep breath, the sweet fragrance of the rain filling the air. *The month of May is so awesome,* she thought, walking cautiously across the slippery grass. *Daylight for another hour yet. Cool.*

By the time she reached the barn, Skye's sneakers had soaked up half of every puddle she encountered. She squeezed in through the door, shut it tightly, and made a beeline to the end stall. Tanya was kneeling on the straw, grooming the filly with a brush and curry comb. The hair in the foal's mane had been arranged like the top of a Trojan helmet.

"Hey," Skye said softly. Tanya and the foal turned their heads toward her. "Well, aren't you two a pair. Her mane looks too cool. Where'd you get that idea?"

79

"I saw it in a horse magazine. It not only looks cool, but it helps keep all that fuzzy mane hair from getting knots and tangles. Do you really like it?" Tanya turned back to her task.

"Yeah, I do," Skye said. "Tanya, did you forget it's time for ensemble practice? All the kids are up there waiting."

Tanya glanced at her watch. "Wow! I completely forgot. I was waiting for someone to call and remind me."

"Mom did call several times, but the rain bouncing off the roof must've drowned out the phone."

"Tell them I'll be up as soon as I finish this."

"But everybody's waiting!"

"They waited for me for thirteen years. They can wait ten more minutes!"

"Tanya!" *You spoiled brat!* "We don't have all night!"

Tanya brushed the foal as though Skye wasn't even there.

"For your own good," Skye's voice softened, "you'd better come up now. You can keep the group waiting, but you better not mess with Mrs. C. If you get grounded now, you'll be out of this barn faster than you can say boo."

"All right, all right, I'm coming," Tanya griped. She stood and stroked the foal on its neck. "Don't go crazy."

Skye started walking away. "I'll tell them you're coming—now! Oh, and I hung your raincoat on the outside of the stall. You'll need it."

Skye walked away, listening for a thank you that never came. She slipped out the barn door and charged back to the house. "Why do I even bother?"

Several minutes later, both Skye and Tanya were in their places, their soaking wet sneakers left at the kitchen door. The group practiced "until their fingers were mush," Bobby said. Mrs. Chambers directed for timing and helped Tanya adjust her pitch and volume to the rest of the group. Finally, as the setting sun peeked out from under the dispersing rain clouds, the ensemble finished the "Lord, Send Me Anywhere" medley for the last time.

"Excellent," Mrs. Chambers said. "You kids did a great job. That piece is ready for the conference. Very nice work."

"Mrs. C.," Morgan said, "can we get the iced tea and brownies out now?"

"Sure," Mrs. Chambers said.

"I'll help," Skye said as she and Morgan headed toward the kitchen.

"Brownies!" Bobby exclaimed, poking at his glasses. "What a noble reward for our hard work."

"Are you sure your mushy fingers can handle a brownie?" Melissa laughed.

"If I know Bobby," Chad said, "he'd grab the brownie with his toes if he had to."

In the kitchen, Morgan opened the refrigerator door. "I'll get the brownies and tea," she said to Skye. "Do you wanna put the napkins and cups on the table? Oh—and grab that bag of chips in the cupboard too."

"Got it," Skye said. She walked to the sink to wash her hands. Outside, the beauty of a setting sun bathed the earth in glistening shades of pink. Her gaze wandered to the right to the picnic grove. It nestled comfortably under towering pines that still bowed with the weight of their rain-soaked branches. Straight ahead, Skye studied the grass in the fenced-in field, each blade a diamond as the sun's rays splashed off the mantle of rain droplets. To the left, the red barn looked even redder, and . . .

Wait! What is that? Skye asked herself. *Is that the neighbor's dog running through our yard again? Hey, that's not a dog! That's a little horse!*

"Oh, no! The foal's outside the barn!" Skye called out, leaning forward on the sink and staring out the window. "She's drenched! She must've been out in all that rain!"

"What!" Morgan motored to the sliding door in the dining room. "Mrs. C., come quick!" she yelled.

"What's wrong?" Mrs. Chambers ran into the room.

"The foal's out, and she's soaking wet," Skye yelled, wiping her hands on her jeans. "We've got to get her in the barn and warmed up. Fast."

"Tanya!" Mrs. Chambers said, turning back to the living room. "The foal was out in all that rain. You must have forgotten to close the barn door."

Tanya ran into the kitchen, fear plastered all over her face. The other kids followed close behind. "I can't remember if I did," she said. Tears welled up in her eyes.

"Well, it looks like you didn't!" Skye snapped as she knelt, forcing on her wet sneakers and wrestling with the laces. "I told you she'd follow you like you were her mother. She's drenched. If we don't get her warmed up soon, she could catch pneumonia."

"Pneumonia!" Tanya shrieked. "That could kill her!"

Skye stood and turned toward the door, but Tanya flew past her and out the door first, without her sneakers. Skye followed, and they ran flat out toward the foal.

"Tanya, wait!" Skye yelled, slowing down. "We've got to approach her easy. She's scared from being in strange surroundings. We don't want her to take off and run out on the road."

Tanya slowed to a walk, creeping slowly in her bare feet on the slippery grass.

"Now just take it easy," Skye said. "You move to her right, and I'll go to the left. We'll try to get her to go back toward the barn."

"Okay," Tanya squeaked, her voice obviously shaken with fear.

"Skye, I'm behind you to your left!" Skye heard Mrs. Chambers yell from the side of the house. "I'll try to block her if she heads up this way toward the road!"

The filly stood a short distance from the barn at the edge of the lawn. Eyes wide with fear, body trembling from the chill of the rain, she watched the two girls approaching. Her beautiful cocoa-colored coat glistened a brownish pink, and her mane and pink halter made her look like a carnival doll. She let out a weak baby-horse whinny, and her ears tipped forward toward the girls.

"Here, baby." Tanya sniffled, hand outstretched as she crept toward the foal. "Come, baby. We won't hurt you."

Skye approached the foal, one careful step at a time, trying not to spook her. She held her arms out like she wanted to give the foal a big hug.

The filly looked at Skye and braced itself, ready to run like the wind.

"Here, baby," Tanya said, closing to within a few feet.

The foal's head jerked toward Tanya. It let out another loud whinny.

The girls froze.

The foal took a step—then another—slowly—carefully—toward Tanya.

In slow motion, Tanya reached out. Her hand inched its way forward and then crept around the tiny halter.

Skye crept her way toward the foal—ever so slowly—then carefully slipped her arms around its neck.

And they had her!

"Whew," Skye breathed out in a whisper. "Let's get her back in the barn. We need to get her dried off quickly."

"Okay," Tanya said, as tears streamed down her face and her whole body shook. Her free hand quivered as it slid down over the foal's rain-soaked back. "I'm so sorry, baby," Tanya wept. "I'm so sorry."

chapter twelve

Three evenings later, Dr. Gonzales knelt with Mr. Chambers over the still form of the foal on a soft bed of straw. Skye, Mrs. Chambers, and Tanya had all lined up inside the stall. Morgan sat in the doorway.

"I'm afraid it's pneumonia," the doctor said, his stethoscope finding its way to the filly's chest and belly. "It'll be a miracle if she makes it."

"No-o-o," Tanya sobbed, burying her face in her hands. "I didn't mean it!"

Skye stood with her arms folded and her heart breaking. *Tanya, this time it was your fault.* Then Skye prayed, *God, please do a miracle so Tanya can see that you're real.*

Mrs. Chambers stood between Tanya and Skye, her arms around their waists. "We'll do everything we can. She could pull through."

"Miracles do happen," Morgan said.

"We'll do our best and leave the rest in the Lord's hands," Mr. Chambers said. "But now she's going to need round the clock care for sure. Tanya—"

"I'll do it, Mr. C.!" Tanya fell to her knees in front of the foal and touched its neck gently. "I'll move right in here with her and make sure she gets all her meds. I'll keep her warm and clean." She wiped her eyes on her sleeves.

"Tomorrow starts the Memorial Day weekend. Tanya can spend all three days with the foal," Mrs. Chambers said.

"And if I have to, I can miss a few days of school next week—no problem," Tanya said, sniffling. "I'll make it up. I promise."

"Oh, we should know by Monday," Dr. Gonzales said. "And I'll be back then to check on her."

"But it's a holiday," Mr. Chambers said.

"Sickness takes no holiday," said the vet. "That's one fact any doctor is resigned to. If I have to work on a holiday, I'll work. Besides, this case is serious. I'll be here at two o'clock sharp. By then, the fever should have broken, if—and that's a big if—she's going to make it."

"Tell me exactly what to do," Tanya cried, "and I'll do it, starting right now."

You could start by learning to close barn doors, Skye wanted to scream. Love her, Mrs. Chambers' words echoed. "Mom, could I move down here with Tanya? Then she'll have company."

"I don't need anybody with me," Tanya said. "I know what to do."

"You can always use help with the foal," Mrs. Chambers said.

"Yeah, even though there aren't any diapers," Morgan added.

"Look, Tanya," Skye said sharply—and then her tone changed, "I'll run errands for you. I can heat the formula, and answer the phone, and I can even bring your meals down."

"You'd do that for me?" Tanya said.

I'd do it for the baby, Skye thought. "Yeah, why not?" she said. *And I'll do it for you too.*

"Wow! Unreal!" Tanya's face displayed welcomed surprise.

In less than an hour, the girls had everything set up in the foal's stall. Each had staked out a corner with her sleeping bag, clip-on reading lamp, books, and a bag full of essential junk. Skye was finishing a snack of pizza and soda.

Not hungry, Tanya sat on the hay, her back against the wall. The foal, its frail body covered with a red horse blanket, lay asleep with its head resting on Tanya's lap. It struggled for every breath. Tanya stroked the filly's neck and dabbed its runny nose with a tissue while she watched her carefully. Skye sat on her sleeping bag, legs crossed, reading the Bible and filling in answers in a devotional guidebook.

"You're really into this religion stuff, aren't you?" Tanya said.

"It's not religion stuff," Skye said softly, thrilled to have the opportunity to share her faith with Tanya. "When I accepted Christ as my Savior, he became my very best friend. He's always there when I need him, like, right now. He can heal that little foal."

"Yeah, but what if he doesn't want to?" Tanya sneered. "That would be just plain cruel. This baby is so helpless!"

"Tanya, it's not God's fault. Don't blame him for your own stupid mistake. We just have to believe he knows what's best for us—and the foal. By the way, when did you give her the last dose of meds?"

"At eight. She took it pretty well. I think her breathing sounds better, don't you?"

"A little. When's her next bottle?"

Tanya blew her nose and looked at her watch. "In an hour. She's not taking bottles well, though. I hope she drinks more than the last time. Until her next feeding, I need to try to finish a report for English class. Hand me my book and stuff. It's all there in the corner near my pillow."

"Sure, no problem," Skye said.

"I try to keep up with my assignments, but it's so hard to concentrate. If anything happens to her, I don't know what I'll do."

"Listen, we're doin' all we can. She'll make it. You'll see."

"Man, I sure hope so. Oh, I forgot. I need the gigantic dictionary up in my room. It's on the top of my book-shelves. Get it for me."

Skye made a face, ready to lash back at Tanya's bossy tone. Instead, she forced a smile and handed Tanya's book and paper to her. "I'll go get your precious dictionary. Don't go away."

"Don't worry. I'm not going anywhere. No matter how long this takes, I'm here until the foal's up on her feet again."

Skye hurried from the barn to the house, where she found Mrs. Chambers sipping coffee at the dining room table. Tip and Ty lay at her feet. "Hi, Honey," she said. "What's up?"

"The queen—oops—I'm sorry—Tanya needs the dictionary from her bedroom."

"Just think of all you're learning," Mrs. Chambers said with a laugh. "If you ever want to start your own maid service, you'll know just what to do."

"Yeah, right." Skye said, heading toward Tanya's room.

Inside, Skye zeroed in on the bookshelves covering most of one wall. They displayed six rows of Tanya's "favorite" books. *There are more here than at the town library!* Skye decided. On the top shelf rested a humongous book.

Skye hurried around the bed and reached up, pulling the dictionary forward and bracing her arms to catch it. As it fell, a much smaller book and a cluster of papers tumbled to the floor.

"Great," Skye said. "More maid service."

She tossed the dictionary on the bed and knelt down, quickly gathering the papers and reaching for the book.

It lay opened, face down. "Five-Year Diary" was printed in gold letters on a burgundy leather cover.

"Wow!" Skye said, picking up the opened book. "Tanya keeps a diary?"

Don't look, Skye told herself, pausing. *It's wrong.* She started to close the book, but her curiosity forced the pages open. Turning the book around, Skye looked down.

What could Tanya ever write that would be of any interest to me? Skye argued. *Oh, go on. No big deal*, she decided and then looked even closer. She smoothed the page, took a deep breath, and read:

"Dear Diary, I'll be ten tomorrow, and I don't even care." Skye stopped and then gawked at the last few words.

Skye read on. "Another week here at Gram's. I hate it. She still blames me for Mom dying. I feel like running away and never coming back. I wish Mother and Father knew how much I hate it here, but they're always too busy."

Skye shut the book, her eyes wandering to a poster mounted on the wall. BOOKS CAN BE SOME OF YOUR BEST FRIENDS, it read. A stack of colorful books in the arms of a laughing elf helped make the point.

Tanya's grandmother blames her for her mother's death? Skye thought. *But why?*

Tentatively, she looked at the book again, sliding the pages open near the center:

"Dear Diary, another August with Aunt Barb, and I hate it here too. If it wasn't for Kenny, I'd split. Aunt Barb always reminds me that if it wasn't for me, her sister would still be here. I can't wait until I'm old enough to leave. I'm never coming back here—ever!"

Wow! So that's why she never calls them or wants to see them! Skye closed the book, laid it on the bed, and looked at the papers still clutched tightly in her hand. The top sheet of notebook paper was blank, so she turned it over. There Skye found a beautiful colored-pencil sketch of a woman who looked like an older Tanya. "That must be her mother," she concluded. Her glance drifted to the bottom. A colored sketch of Southern Belle graced the page. In the center of the paper Skye read:

"My precious one,
How my arms ache
To touch you—
To hold you—
To love you.
To leave you
Was not my choosing,
Nor was it your cause.
My precious one
I love you.
Mom

Skye's heart raced as though she had just discovered a bag full of gold. But now her mind filled with confusion and shame—not only for what she had discovered but also for what she had done. Her eyes surveyed the space under Tanya's bed, debating whether she should crawl into it. For what seemed like forever, Skye sat still, thinking about Tanya and her mother—and the feelings she had about her own mom. Tears flooded her eyes, and her cheeks flushed hot. *Tanya really does need love and understanding, more than anyone could ever know,* Skye told herself. *But I didn't know!*

Skye stood, confused emotions ripping her insides to shreds. With strong resolve, she worked quickly to clean up the mess, shuffling the papers in her hands into a neat pile. But without giving it a thought, she pulled a second paper from the pile and drew it in front of her face.

Someone had sketched a colored picture of Tanya on the page. At the bottom, there was a beautiful drawing of Belle's new foal. In the center, Tanya had written these words:

"My darling mother,
How my heart aches
To see you—
To touch you—
To know you.
My birth caused your death,
And my life is so empty
Without you.
With my whole heart
I love you,
The child you never knew."

"I can't believe this!" Skye murmured aloud.

"You can't believe what?" Mrs. Chambers said from the doorway.

Skye's nerves jumped like she had sat on hot coals.

"What's going on in here, Honey?"

Tears pricking at the corners of her eyes, Skye slowly faced Mrs. Chambers. "Mom, I know I shouldn't have done it, but her diary was lying wide open—and all these papers—and—and—" Skye's rambling drifted into loud sniffles.

Mrs. Chambers walked in and sat on the edge of the bed. "And you couldn't resist looking?"

Skye refocused on the papers that her hand still clutched. "I know I deserve to be grounded, but I don't care about that. She hates herself, Mom. Her aunt and gram blame her for her mother's death. That's why she went off the deep end when Belle died. She saw herself in that little foal."

"I know, Skye. Right now Tanya's the main topic of discussion here. This past week she started to open up about all of this at Maranatha. She's a troubled young lady. I just got off the phone with her parents. They'll be here on Monday to surprise Tanya. It seems like this might be the perfect time for a Bell family pow wow."

"Mom, look at these beautiful pictures! I didn't know she could draw, and she has really neat poetry here about her feelings." Skye held the papers toward Mrs. Chambers.

Mrs. Chambers held up her hand and stood. "No, Skye, these are part of Tanya's private life. Put them back where you found them. Then come out to the dining room where we can talk more about it. And you need to get back down there. She's probably wondering where you are."

"Do you think I should tell her that I saw this stuff?" Skye asked, wiping her eyes.

"Let's go pray about it," Mrs. Chambers said. "Then you'll know."

ow's our baby doing this fine holiday?" Morgan smiled in the doorway of the foal's box stall. Morning sunlight streamed in through the window in the tack room behind her, making her red hair glow.

Tanya sat at her station on the straw, stroking the filly's neck. The foal, now without its blanket, lay sound asleep. "She's breathing much better, isn't she, Skye?" Tanya said cheerfully.

"Yeah," Skye said, reading in her corner. "Her nose isn't runny anymore, and she's taking her bottles much better too. Even though she's too weak to stand, I think she's gonna make it."

"That's great," Morgan said, starting to back away. "I'm truckin' to the picnic grove to help Mom and Dad get ready for lunch. Oh, I almost forgot. Mrs. C. wants to know if you guys want hot dogs or hamburgers."

"I'm not big on either one," Tanya said. "If they don't have anything better, I'll just take a baked potato."

Slamming her book shut, Skye looked at Tanya and just shook her head. "Tell Mom I'll take one of each."

"Okay!" Morgan's voice trailed off as she headed out of the barn. "And I can't wait to tell them the good news about the baby ... God does work miracles ... catch you later!"

"I don't get it!" Tanya said. "Why is she so happy all the time? She drives me crazy with her constant smiling. If I were sitting in that chair, I'd let the whole world know what a bum deal I got. Where are her parents? Yeah, and while we're on parents, where are yours? Nobody ever told me any of this stuff."

"You never gave us the chance," Skye said. "We tried to tell you. Morgan's parents are divorced, and her mom has a bunch of other kids, so Morgan doesn't see her much. Her dad's remarried and in California, I think."

"That's tough," Tanya said in a sincere tone.

"Now, my parents are a whole other disaster. I don't have a clue where they are. They stuck me in foster care when I was little."

"I know a few foster kids in Philly. Some like their foster homes, and some don't."

"I've been in about fifteen different ones, I think." Skye looked over at Tanya. "Some of them were the pits, but this one has been the best. I never want to leave here. Mom and Dad Chambers really love me. I can tell. And you're so lucky that you already have two parents who care about you, and—"

"Well, I still don't get it. Both you and Morgan have been handed a raw deal, the way I see it. Why are you so la-la happy all the time?"

"Tanya, it's because God is with us," Skye said, sitting on her haunches. "When you accept him as your Savior, he helps you with all your problems. And the Bible says that when you trust in him, he promises you eternal life in heaven. Now that's something to be happy about."

"I wish I could be happy." Tanya stared at the wall.

"You can!" Skye bubbled. "Don't you ever feel like you need God to help you? And don't you ever feel sorry for all the rotten things you've done? God's ready to forgive and forget."

Tanya stared at the foal and ran her fingers through its fuzzy mane. "Well, once in a while I feel bad about something I've done, but then I block it out of my mind."

"You can't block it out forever," Skye said. Then her own conscience took her back to Tanya's bedroom. "Speaking of rotten things, I have to tell you something."

"What?"

"Well—and I'm super sorry about this—but the other night when I went to get your dictionary, your diary and some papers fell on the floor—and—well—I accidentally on purpose looked at them. I'm really sorry. I didn't mean it."

Tanya's face melted into a nasty scowl. "And what exactly did you see?" she barked.

"Only that your aunt and gram blame you for your mom's death. And I saw those really neat pictures you drew—and some cool poetry about your mother. But I'm really sorry."

Tanya's eyes threw pitchforks at Skye. "Hey, you had no business looking at that stuff. Doesn't a person have any privacy around here?"

Skye felt her face flush with embarrassment. "Tanya, I told you it was, sort of, an accident. I don't go around snooping in other kids' rooms. You did give me permission to go in there."

"Yeah, to get a dictionary, not to read about my whole life," Tanya sassed. "I'm going to tell Mr. and Mrs. Chambers. And I hope you get grounded for life!"

"I already did tell Mom everything," Skye confessed. "And I am grounded, but not for life. I got two weeks starting tomorrow. So you'll be on your own down here for a while with the filly."

"That should teach you a good lesson," Tanya said, her tone softening. Deep in thought, she settled back against the wall. "Well, I guess it wasn't such a major crime after all. Just so you didn't read my diary from cover to cover. That would have made me furious."

"And it won't ever happen again. I promise," Skye said, glancing at her watch. "Hey, lunch should be ready soon," she said, glad to change the subject. "Are you gonna come out with us, or should I— "

The foal let out a soft nicker, and the girls froze in their spots.

Slowly, the foal raised its head and placed it back down. Then in a jerking motion, she struggled to get up. She tried several times and finally managed to sit with her four legs folded underneath, her eyes wide with wonder.

Tanya scrambled to her knees and whispered, "I think she wants to stand."

Skye crawled on her hands and knees to the filly. "Let's help her. Now take it easy. She looks a little scared. You wrap your arms around her neck, and I'll slip my arms around her belly. If she makes the least little effort, just urge her up."

"Okay," Tanya said, her eyes glued to the foal.

The tiny horse let out a louder nicker. With all the strength she could muster, she stretched her front legs out and pushed upward with her wobbly back legs. The girls placed their arms around her, gently urging the foal upward. The filly braced itself on all fours, wobbling like her legs were made of paper. The girls held on, and in a few moments, the foal stood with her legs planted firmly in the straw. She let out a loud baby-horse whinny, and the girls joined in a celebration of smiles and giggles, their eyes filled with wonder!

"She's up!" Skye said. "Tanya, she's up! She's gonna make it! Aw! Sweet!"

Then it happened again. With her arms still draped around the foal, Tanya started to cry.

Skye quickly stood. "Tanya, what's wrong now? Are you okay?"

Tanya released the foal and slumped back into her corner. Pulling her knees tightly against her chest, she buried her face in her arms. She sobbed as though the foal had died right there on that very spot.

Skye held the filly by its halter and stroked its soft warm back. *God, show me what to do!* she prayed.

"I hate my mother for leaving me!" Tanya wailed, never looking up. "I hate her!"

Skye patted the filly on its neck. "Good baby," she said, quietly slipping down next to Tanya.

"Why did she have to die?" Tanya said louder. "I hate her! And I hate the Bells too. They just don't understand."

"I hated my mother too," Skye said softly, "but I don't anymore."

The barn was silent except for Tanya's sobs.

"You hated your mother?" Tanya finally said, looking up. "And you don't anymore?"

"God took all that hate and bitterness from me, Tanya. He can do that for you too. Just give all your heartache to Jesus."

Tanya buried her face in her arms and cried even harder.

Gently, Skye slipped her arm around Tanya. The thought of her own mother ran through Skye's mind, filling her eyes with tears. "God can help you. Just let him."

"Skye, I believe you," Tanya said, sobbing. "This is all starting to make sense now, especially what you and Mrs. Chambers have told me about God. I'd like to invite Jesus into my heart. He can change me and help me through this. I just know it."

During the next moments, Skye shared with Tanya the glorious message of Jesus Christ and his plan of salvation. Tanya listened to every word and pouring her heart out, she asked him to forgive her sins and come into her life. When Tanya finished, Skye prayed, asking the Lord to take Tanya's bitterness away.

"Amen," Skye said, standing. "Tanya, what you just did is a God thing. He'll change you on the inside, and before long it will show on the outside."

"You know, I feel better already." Tanya smiled. "Much better."

"We girls always feel better after a good cry," Skye said, "and this time, God helped. More than we'll ever know. And God helped our little baby too."

Both girls turned their attention back to the foal.

With wobbling legs, the filly took several steps forward, reaching its soft nose toward Tanya. It licked her hands like they were pure sugar, gave a sassy snort, and then let out a long high-pitched baby-horse whinny.

"She is so awesome!" Tanya giggled through her tears. "And so is God!"

"Hey, let's take her outside!" Skye said. "It's really warm and sunny, and there's no breeze! She'll love soakin' up the rays. We'll take her over to the picnic grove and show her to Mom and Dad."

"Okay. And I'd like to tell everybody what I just did with God too," Tanya said. She jumped to her feet, grabbed a bright pink lead rope from a hook, and clipped it to the foal's halter. "Let's go," she said.

The girls slowly led the foal out of the barn and made their way across the field toward the pavilion.

"Skye, do you think Mr. and Mrs. C. have a name picked out for her yet?" Tanya rambled on. "Could you get me one of those devotionals like you have—and I'll need a Bible, won't I?"

Skye struggled to get a word in edgewise. "As of last night, Mom said they didn't have a name yet—and yes, we can get you a Bible and a devotional—and—who is that over there with Mom and Dad?"

Tanya turned and looked. "Hey," she said, "that looks like—it is! It's Mother and Father! Here, Skye, watch the baby." She shoved the lead rope into Skye's hands and took off toward the grove.

"Sure! No problem!" Skye laughed.

"Mother! Father!" Tanya yelled.

Tanya's parents turned and hurried toward their daughter. Tanya ran across the bridge, past the gazebo, and fell into their welcoming arms.

As Skye coaxed the foal along, Tippy and Tyler ran to greet her. Then all four joined the group now gathering in the grove. As usual, Tanya was crying, but this time, Skye knew it was different.

Tanya clung to her mother and cried deep sobs that rendered Dr. Bell wide-eyed and speechless.

Mr. Bell, as well, displayed a strange combination of pleasant surprise and total shock. "Baby, what's the matter?"

"Nothing," Tanya answered, giving her father an extra long hug before stepping back. "For once, everything is okay. I have so much to tell you." She turned and looked at Skye with the foal. "The filly is gonna be all right. Did you know she was sick, and it was my fault?"

"Yes," Dr. Bell said. "Mr. Chambers told us."

"But it's because of Tanya's care that she pulled through," Mrs. Chambers said. "She hasn't let her out of her sight for three days."

"Skye helped too," Tanya said. "And so did prayer."

"What?" Mr. Bell said.

"Like I said, Father, I have tons to tell you."

"You both look like you've been crying buckets," Morgan said to the girls. "What happened?"

"That's part of what Tanya has to tell everybody," Skye said. "Wait until you hear this!"

Mr. Chambers adjusted his chef's hat and raised a grill spatula. "Ladies and gentlemen, I'd like to say something before we indulge ourselves with this luscious picnic. May I have your attention? Tanya, I think you're going to like this."

"What?" Tanya asked.

"We've decided to let you name this little filly. Would you like that?"

"You mean it, Mr. C.?" Tanya's face beamed.

"Yes, we think since you've sacrificed so much time to help her, it's only right. What do you say?" Mrs. Chambers said.

"Wow! That's awesome," Tanya said. "Give me a few minutes. I want to think about it."

"You don't have to name her right now!" Morgan giggled.

"No, you'll have lots of time," Mr. Bell added.

"What do you mean?" Tanya said.

Skye offered the lead rope to Tanya.

Tanya retrieved the rope and slipped her hand around the filly's halter.

Skye studied the tightly knit circle. Smiles radiated from every face, waiting for her next few words.

"She's yours, Tanya," Skye announced. "Since you'll soon be living on a farm—she's yours."

"No way!" Tanya practically screamed. She knelt down and wrapped her arms around the foal's neck. "You mean it? She's mine? Are you serious?"

"You two look like peas in a pod," Dr. Bell said. "Tanya, your father and I want you to be happy."

"Oh, Mother—I am happy—really happy, but it's mostly because I invited Jesus into my heart today."

"You did?" Dr. Bell said.

"Well, Baby, that's real nice," Mr. Bell added. "We're glad you did it."

"When did this happen?" Mrs. Chambers asked.

"Just now in the barn," Skye said. "We prayed together and everything."

"I have so much to tell you all," Tanya said, still hugging the foal. "I feel so different, so free—hey—I've got it! How's this for a name? Let's call her Liberty—Liberty Belle—because I feel so free."

"That's an excellent name," Mr. Chambers said.

"Just perfect," Mrs. Chambers agreed.

"Too sweet," Morgan added.

"That is very cool!" Skye said, smiling. "And Tanya, you are pretty cool yourself!"

A Letter to my Keystone Stables Fans

Dear Reader,

Are you crazy about horses like I am? Are you fortunate enough to have a horse now, or are you dreaming about the day when you will have one of your very own?

I've been crazy about horses ever since I can remember. When I was a child, I lived where I couldn't have a horse. Even if I had lived in the country, my folks didn't have the money to buy me one. So, as I grew up in a small coal town in central Pennsylvania, I dreamed about horses and collected horse pictures and horse models. I drew horse pictures and wrote horse stories, and I read every horse book I could get my hands on.

For Christmas when I was ten, I received a leather-fringed western jacket and a cowgirl hat. Weather permitting, I wore them when I walked to and from school. On the way, I imagined that I was riding a gleaming white steed into a world of mountain trails and forest paths.

Occasionally, during the summer, my mother took me to a riding academy where I rode a horse for one hour at a time. I always rubbed my hands (and hard!) on my mount before we left the ranch. For the rest of the day I tried not to wash my hands so I could smell the horse and remember the great time I had. Of course, I never could sit at the dinner table without Mother first sending me to the faucet to get rid of that "awful stench."

To get my own horse, I had to wait until I grew up, married, and bought a home in the country with enough land for a barn and a pasture. Moon Doggie, my very first horse, was a handsome brown and white pinto Welsh Mountain Pony. Many other equines came to live at our place where, in later years, my husband and I also opened our hearts to foster kids who needed a caring home. Most of the kids loved the horses as much as I did.

Although owning horses and rearing foster kids are now in my past, I fondly remember my favorite steed, who has long since passed from the scene. Rex, part Quarter Horse and part Tennessee Walker, was a 14 ½ hands-high bay. Rex was the kind of horse every kid dreams about. With a smooth walking gait, he gave me a thrilling ride every time I climbed into the saddle. Yet, he was so gentle,

Rex

a young child could sit confidently on his back. Rex loved sugar cubes and nuzzled my pockets to find them. When cleaning his hooves, all I had to do was touch the target leg, and he lifted his hoof into my waiting hands. Rex was my special horse, and although he died at the ripe old age of twenty-five many years ago, I still miss him.

If you have a horse now or just dream about the day when you will, I beg you to do all you can to learn how to treat with tender love and respect one of God's most beautiful creatures. Horses make wonderful pets, but they require much more attention than a dog or a cat. For their loyal devotion to you, they only ask that you love them in return with the proper food, a clean barn, and the best of care.

Although Southern Belle's story that you just read is fiction, the following pages contain horse facts that any horse lover will enjoy. It is my desire that these pages will help you to either care for your own horse better now or prepare you for that moment when you'll be able to throw your arms around that one special horse of your dreams that you can call your very own.

Happy riding!
Marsha Hubler

Are You Ready to Own Your First Horse?

The most exciting moment in any horse lover's life is to look into the eyes of a horse she can call her very own. No matter how old you are when you buy your first horse, it's hard to match the thrill of climbing onto his back and taking that first ride on a woodsy trail or dusty road that winds through open fields. A well-trained mount will give you a special friendship and years of pleasure as you learn to work with him and become a confident equestrian team.

But owning a horse involves much more than hopping on his back, racing him into a lather of sweat, and putting him back in his stall until you're ready to ride him again.

If you have your own horse now, you've already realized that caring for a horse takes a great amount of time and money. Besides feeding him twice a day, you must also groom him, clean his stall, "pick" his hooves, and have a farrier (a horseshoe maker and applier) and veterinarian make regular visits.

If you don't own a horse and you are begging your parents to buy one, please realize that you can't keep the horse in your garage and just feed him grass cuttings left over from a mowed lawn. It is a sad fact that too many neglected horses have ended up in rescue shelters after well-meaning families did not know how to properly care for their steeds.

If you feel that you are ready to have your own horse, please take time to answer the following questions. If you say yes to all of them, then you are well on your way to being the proud owner of your very own mount.

1. Do you have the money to purchase:

   - the horse? (A good grade horse can start at $800. Registered breeds can run into the thousands.)
   - a saddle, pad, and bridle, and a winter blanket or raincoat? ($300+ brand new)
   - a hard hat (helmet) and riding boots? ($150+)
   - essentials such as coat and hoof conditioner, bug repellent, electric clipper and grooming kit, saddle soap, First Aid kit, and vitamins? ($150+)

2. Does your family own at least a one-stall shed or barn and at least two acres of grass (enough pasture for one horse) to provide adequate grazing for your horse during warm months? If not, do you have the money to regularly purchase quality oats and alfalfa/timothy hay, and do you have the place to store the hay? Oh, and let's not forget the constant supply of sawdust or straw you need for stall bedding!

3. Are you ready to get up early enough every day to give your horse a bucket of fresh water, feed him a coffee can full of oats and one or two sections of clean dry hay (if you have no pasture), and "muck out" the manure from the barn?

4. Every evening, are you again ready to water and feed your horse, clean the barn, groom him, and pick his hooves?
5. Will you ride him at least twice a week, weather permitting?
6. If the answer to any of the above questions is no, then does your family have the money to purchase a horse and board him at a nearby stable? (Boarding fees can run as high as a car payment. Ask your parents how much that is.)

So, there you have the bare facts about owning and caring for a horse. If you don't have your own horse yet, perhaps you'll do as I did when I was young: I read all the books I could about horses. I analyzed all the facts about the money and care needed to make a horse happy. Sad as it made me feel, I finally realized that I would have to wait until I was much older to assume such a great responsibility. And now years later, I can look back and say, "For the horse's sake, I'm very glad I did wait."

I hope you've made the decision to give your horse the best possible TLC that you can. That might mean improving his care now or waiting until you're older to get a horse of your own. Whatever you and your parents decide, please remember that the result of your efforts should be a happy horse. If that's the case, you will be happy too.

Let's Go Horse Shopping!

If you are like I was when I was younger, I dreamed of owning the most beautiful horse in the world. My dream horse, with his long-flowing mane and wavy tail dragging on the ground, would arch his neck and prance with only a touch of my hand on his withers or a gentle rub of my boot heel on his barrel. My dream horse was often different colors. Sometimes he was silvery white; other times he was jet black. He was often a pinto blend of the deepest chocolate browns, blacks, and whites. No matter what color he was, he always took me on a perfect ride, responding to my slightest commands.

When I was old enough to be responsible to care for my own steed, I already knew that the horse of my dreams was just that, the horse of my dreams. To own a prancing pure white stallion or a high-stepping coal-black mare, I would have to buy a Lipizzaner, American Saddle Horse, or an Andalusian. But those kinds of horses were either not for sale to a beginner with a tiny barn or they cost so much, I couldn't afford one. I was amazed to discover that there are about 350 different breeds of horses, and I had to look for a horse that was just right for me, possibly even a good grade horse (that means not registered) that was a safe mount. Color really didn't matter as long as the horse was healthy and gave a safe, comfortable ride. (But I'm not sure what my friends might have said if I had a purple horse. That certainly would have been a "horse of a different color!") Then I had to decide if I wanted to ride western or English style. Well, living in central Pennsylvania farm country with oodles of trails and dirt roads, the choice for me was simple: western.

I'm sure if you don't have your own horse yet, you've dreamed and thought a lot about what your first horse will be. Perhaps you've already had a horse, but now you're thinking of buying another one. What kind should you get?

Let's look at some of the breeds that are the most popular for both western and English riders today. We'll briefly trace a few breeds' roots and characteristics while you decide if that kind of horse might be the one for you. Please keep in mind that this information speaks to generalities of the breeds. If given the proper care and training, most any breeds of horses make excellent mounts as well.

Some Popular Breeds (Based on Body Confirmation)

The Arabian

Sometimes called "The China Doll of the Horse Kingdom," the Arabian is known as the most beautiful of horse breeds because of its delicate features. Although research indicates Arabians are the world's oldest and purest breed, it is not known whether they originated in Arabia. However, many Bible scholars believe that the first horse that God created in the Garden of Eden must have embodied the strength and beauty that we see in the Arabian horse of today. It is also believed that all other breeds descended from this gorgeous breed that has stamina as well as courage and intelligence.

A purebred Arabian has a height of only 14 or 15 hands, a graceful arch in his neck, and a high carriage in his tail. It is easy to identify one of these horses by examining his head. If you see a small, delicate "dish" face with a broad forehead and tiny muzzle, two ears that point inward and large eyes that are often ringed in black, you are probably looking at an Arabian. The breed comes in all colors, (including dappled and some paint), but if you run your finger against the grain of any pureblood Arabian's coat, you will see an underlying bed of black skin. Perhaps that's why whites are often called "grays."

Generally, Arabians are labeled spirited and skittish, even though they might have been well trained. If you have your heart set on buying an Arabian, make sure you first have the experience to handle a horse that, although he might be loyal, will also want to run with the wind.

The Morgan

The Morgan Horse, like a Quarter Horse (see below), can explode into a gallop for a short distance. The Morgan, with its short legs, muscles, and fox ears, also looks very much like the Quarter Horse. How can we tell the two breeds apart?

A Morgan is chunkier than a Quarter Horse, especially in his stout neck. His long, wavy tail often flows to the ground. His trot is quick and short and with such great stamina, he can trot all day long.

So where are the Morgan's roots?

The horse breed was named after Justin Morgan, a frail music teacher who lived in Vermont at the turn of the eighteenth century. Instead of receiving cash for a debt owed, Mr. Morgan was given two colts. The smallest one, which he called Figure, was an undersized dark bay with a black mane and tail. Mr. Morgan sold the one colt, but he kept Figure, which he thought was a cross between a Thoroughbred and an Arabian. Over the years, he found the horse to be strong enough to pull logs and fast enough to beat Thoroughbreds in one afternoon and eager to do it all over again the same day!

When Mr. Morgan died, his short but powerful horse was called "Justin Morgan" in honor of his owner. After that, all of Justin Morgan's foals were called Morgans. The first volume of the Morgan Horse Register was published in 1894. Since then, hundreds of thousands of Morgans have been registered.

If you go Morgan hunting, you will find the breed in any combination of blacks, browns, and whites. Don't look for a tall horse because all Morgans are between 14 and 15 hands tall, just right for beginners. If you're fortunate enough to find a well-trained Morgan, he'll give you years of pleasure whether you ask him to gallop down a country trail, pull a wagon, or learn to jump obstacles.

The Mustang

If you want a taste of America's Wild West from days gone by, then you should treat yourself to the "Wild Horse of America," the Mustang.

This 14–15 hand, stout horse has its roots from Cortez and the Spanish conquistadors from the sixteenth century.

Although the Mustang's name comes from the Spanish word, *mesteno*, which means "a stray or wild grazer," he is most well known as the horse of the Native Americans. Numerous tribes all over the western plains captured horses that had escaped from their Spanish owners and ran wild. The Native Americans immediately claimed the Mustang as a gift from their gods and showed the world that the horse was, and is, easy to train once domesticated.

It didn't take long for the white settlers to discover the versatility of the Mustang. Because of his endurance, this little horse soon became a favorite for the Pony Express, the U.S. cavalry, cattle round-ups, and caravans.

Since the 1970s, the U.S. Bureau of Land Management has stepped in to save the Mustangs from extinction. As a result, herds of Mustangs still roam freely in U.S. western plains today. At different times of the year and in different parts of the country, the Adopt-a-Horse-or-Burro Program allows horse lovers to take a Mustang or burro home for a year and train it to be a reliable mount. After the year, the eligible family can receive a permanent ownership title from the government. As of October 2007, more than 218,000 wild horses and burros have been placed into private care since the adoption program began in 1973.

If you'd like a "different" kind of horse that sometimes has a scrubby look but performs with the fire of the Arab-barb blood, then go shopping for a Mustang. You'll find him in any black, brown, or white combination and with the determination and stamina to become your best equine friend.

The Quarter Horse

There's no horse lover anywhere in the world who hasn't heard of the American Quarter Horse. In fact, the Quarter Horse is probably the most popular breed in the United States today.

But what exactly is a Quarter Horse? Is he only a quarter of a horse in size, therefore, just a pony? No, this fantastic breed isn't a quarter of anything!

The Quarter Horse originated in American colonial times in Virginia when European settlers bred their stout English workhorses with the Native Americans' Mustangs. The result? A short-legged but muscular equine with a broad head and little "fox" ears, a horse that has great strength and speed.

It didn't take long for the colonists and Native Americans to discover that their new crossbreed was the fastest piece of horseflesh in the world for a quarter of a mile. Thus, the breed was christened the American Quarter Horse and began to flourish. Besides running quick races, it also pulled wagons, canal boats, and plows. When the American West opened up, cowpokes discovered that the Quarter Horse was perfect for herding cattle and to help rope steers. Although it remained a distinct breed for over three hundred years in the U.S., the Quarter Horse was only recognized with its own studbook in 1941.

If you are looking for a reliable mount that has a comfortable trot and smooth gallop, you might want to look at some *seasoned* Quarter Horses. (That means they have been trained properly and are at least five or six years old.) They come in any color or combination of colors. Their temperament is generally friendly, yet determined to get the job done that you ask them to do.

The Shetland Pony

Many beginning riders incorrectly believe that the smaller the horse, the easier it is to control him. You might be thinking, "I'm tiny, so I need a tiny horse!" But many beginners have found out the hard way that a Shetland Pony is sometimes no piece of cake.

Shetland Ponies originated as far back as the Bronze Age in the Shetland Isles, northeast of mainland Scotland.

Research has found that they are related to the ancient Scandinavian ponies. Shetland Ponies were first used for pulling carts, carrying peat and other items, and plowing farmland. Thousands of Shetlands also worked as "pit ponies," pulling coal carts in British mines in the mid–nineteenth century. The Shetland found its way at the same time to the United States when they were imported to also work in mines.

The American Shetland Pony Club was founded in 1888 as a registry to keep the pedigrees for all the Shetlands that were being imported from Europe at that time.

Shetlands are usually only 10.2 hands or shorter. They have a small head, sometimes with a dished face, big Bambi eyes, and small ears. The original breed has a short, muscular neck, stocky bodies, and short, strong legs. Shetlands can give you a bouncy ride because of their short broad backs and deep girths. These ponies have long thick manes and tails, and in winter climates their coats of any color can grow long and fuzzy.

If you decide you'd like to own a Shetland, spend a great deal of time looking for one that is mild mannered. Because of past years of hard labor, the breed now shows a dogged determination that often translates into stubbornness. So be careful, and don't fall for that sweet, fuzzy face without riding the pony several times before you buy him. You might get a wild, crazy ride from a "shortstuff" mount that you never bargained for!

The Tennessee Walking Horse

If you buy a Tennessee Walker, get ready for a thrilling ride as smooth as running water!

The Tennessee Walking Horse finds its roots in 1886 in Tennessee, when a Standardbred (a Morgan and Standardbred trotter cross) stallion named Black Allan refused to trot; instead, he chose to amble or "walk" fast. With effortless speed comparable to other horses' trots,

112

Black Allan's new gait (each hoof hitting the ground at a different time) amazed the horse world. Owners of Thoroughbreds and saddle horses were quick to breed their mares to this delightful new "rocking-horse" stud, and the Tennessee Walker was on its way to becoming one of the most popular breeds in the world. In just a few short years, the Walker became the favorite mount of not only circuit-riding preachers and plantation owners, but ladies riding sidesaddle as well.

Today the Walker, which comes in any black, brown, or white color or combination, is a versatile horse and is comfortable when ridden English or Western. He is usually 15 to 17 hands tall and has a long neck and sloping shoulders. His head is large but refined, and he has small ears. Because he has a short back, his running walk, for which he is known, comes naturally.

If you go shopping for a Tennesee Walker, you will find a horse that is usually mild mannered yet raring to go. Although most walkers are big and you might need a stepstool to climb on one, you will be amazed at how smooth his walk and rocking-horse canter is. In fact, you might have trouble making yourself get off!

Some Popular Breeds (Based on Body Color)

The Appaloosa

French cave paintings thousands of years old have "spotted" horses among its subjects, ancient China had labeled their spotted horses as "heavenly," and Persians have called their spotted steeds "sacred." Yet the spotted Appaloosa breed that we know today is believed to have originated in the northwestern Native Americans tribe called the Nez Perce in the seventeenth century.

When colonists expanded the United States territory westward, they found a unique people who lived near the Palouse River (which runs from north central Idaho to the Snake River in southeast Washington State). The Nez

Perce Indian tribe had bred a unique horse—red or blue roans with white spots on the rump. Fascinated, the colonists called the beautiful breed *palousey*, which means "the stream of the green meadows." Gradually, the name changed to *Appaloosa*.

The Nez Perce people lost most of their horses following the end of the Nez Perce War in 1877, and the breed started to decline for several decades. However, a small number of dedicated Appaloosa lovers kept the breed alive. Finally, a breed registry was formed in 1938. The Appaloosa was named the official state horse of Idaho in 1975.

If you decide to buy an Appaloosa, you'll own one of the most popular breeds in the United States today. It is best known as a stock horse used in a number of western riding events, but it's also seen in many other types of equestrian contests as well. So if you would like to ride English or Western, or want to show your horse or ride him on a mountain trail, an Appaloosa could be just the horse for you.

Appaloosas can be any solid base color, but the gorgeous blanket of spots that sometimes cover the entire horse identifies the special breed. Those spotted markings are not the same as pintos or the "dapple grays" and some other horse colors. For a horse to be registered as a pureblood Appaloosa, it also has to have striped hooves, white outer coat (sclera) encircling its brown or blue eyes, and mottled (spotted) skin around the eyes and lips. The Appaloosa is one of the few breeds to have skin mottling, and so this characteristic is a surefire way of identifying a true member of the breed.

In 1983, the Appaloosa Horse Club in America decided to limit the crossbreeding of Appaloosas to only three main confirmation breeds: the Arabian, the American Quarter Horse, and the Thoroughbred. Thus, the Appaloosa color breed also became a true confirmation breed as well.

If you want your neighbors to turn their heads your way when you ride past, then look for a well-trained Appaloosa. Most registered "Apps" are 15 hands or shorter but are full of muscle and loaded with spots. Sometimes, though, it takes several years for an Appaloosa's coat to mature to its full color. So if it's color you're looking for, shop for a seasoned App!

The Pinto

The American Pinto breed has its origins in the wild Mustang of the western plains. The seventeenth and eighteenth century Native Americans bred color into their "ponies," using them for warhorses and prizing those with the richest colors. When the "Westward Ho" pioneers captured wild Mustangs with flashy colors, they bred them to all different breeds of European stock horses. Thus, the Pinto has emerged as a color breed, which includes all different body shapes and sizes today.

The Pinto Horse Association of America was formed in 1956, although the bloodlines of many Pintos can be traced three or four generations before then. The association doesn't register Appaloosas, draft breeds, or horses with mule roots or characteristics. Today more than 100,000 Pintos are registered throughout the U.S., Canada, Europe, and Asia.

Pintos have a dark background with random patches of white and have two predominant color patterns:

1. Tobiano (Toe-bee-ah'-no) Pintos are white with large spots of brown or black color. Spots can cover much of the head, chest, flank, and rump, often including the tail. Legs are generally white, which makes the horse look like he's white with flowing spots of color. The white usually crosses the center of the back of the horse.

115

2. Overo (O-vair'-o) Pintos are colored horses with jagged white markings that originate on the animal's side or belly and spread toward the neck, tail, legs, and back. The deep, rich browns or blacks appear to frame the white. Thus, Overos often have dark backs and dark legs. Horses with bald or white faces are often Overos. Their splashy white markings on the rest of their body make round, lacy patterns.

Perhaps you've heard the term *paint* and wonder if that kind of horse is the same as a Pinto. Well, amazingly, the two are different breeds! A true Paint horse (registered by the American Paint Horse Association) must be bred from pureblood Paints, Quarter Horses, or Thoroughbreds. The difference in eligibility between the two registries has to do with the bloodlines of the horse, not its color or pattern.

So if you're shopping for a flashy mount and you don't care about a specific body type of horse, then set your sites on a Pinto or Paint. You might just find a well-trained registered or grade horse that has the crazy colors you've been dreaming about for a very long time!

The Palomino

No other color of horse will turn heads his way than the gorgeous golden Palomino. While the average person thinks the ideal color for a Palomino is like a shiny gold coin, the Palomino breed's registry allows all kinds of coat colors as long as the mane and tail are silvery white. A white blaze can be on the face but can't extend beyond the eyes. The Palomino can also have white stockings, but the white can't extend beyond the knees. Colors of Palominos can range from a deep, dark chocolate to an almost-white cremello. As far as body confirmation, four breeds are strongly represented in crossbreeding with the

Palomino today: the American Saddlebred, Tennessee Walker, Morgan, and Quarter Horse.

No one is sure where the Palomino came from, but it is believed that the horse came from Spain. An old legend says that Isabella, queen of Spain in the late fifteenth century, loved her golden horses so much she sent one stallion and five mares across the Atlantic to start thriving in the New World. Eventually those six horses lived in what is now Texas and New Mexico, where Native Americans captured the horses' offspring and incorporated them into their daily lives. From those six horses came all the Palominos in the United States, which proves how adaptable the breed is in different climates.

Today you can find Palominos all over the world and involved in all kinds of settings from jumping to ranching to rodeos. One of their most popular venues is pleasing crowds in parades, namely the Tournament of Roses Parade in Pasadena, California, every New Year's Day.

Perhaps you've dreamed of owning a horse that you could be proud of whether you are trail riding on a dirt road, showing in a western pleasure class, or strutting to the beat of a band in a parade. If that's the case, then the Palomino is the horse for you!

If you're shopping for the best in bloodlines, look for a horse that has a double registry! With papers that show the proper bloodlines, an Appaloosa Quarter Horse can be double registered. Perhaps you'd like a palomino Morgan or a pinto Tennessee Walker?

Who Can Ride a Horse?

As you have read this book about Skye, Morgan, and some of the other children with special needs, perhaps you could identify with one in particular. Do you have what society calls a handicap or disability? Do you use a wheelchair? Do you have any friends who are blind or have autism? Do you or your friends with special needs believe that none of you could ever ride a horse?

Although Keystone Stables is a fictitious place, there are real ranches and camps that connect horses with children just like Skye and Morgan, Sooze in book two, Tanya in book three, Jonathan in book four, Katie in book five, Joey in book six, and Wanda in book seven. That special kind of treatment and interaction has a long complicated name called Equine Facilitated Psychotherapy (EFP.)

EFP might include handling and grooming the horse, lunging, riding, or driving a horse-drawn cart. In an EFP program, a licensed mental health professional works together with a certified horse handler. Sometimes one EFP person can have the credentials for both. Whatever the case, the professionals are dedicated to helping both the child and the horse learn to work together as a team.

Children with autism benefit greatly because of therapeutic riding. Sometimes a child who has never been able to speak or "connect" with another person, even a parent, will bond with a horse in such a way that the child learns to relate to other people or starts to talk.

An author friend has told me of some of her family members who've had experience with horses and autistic children. They tell a story about a mute eight-year-old boy who was taking therapeutic treatment. One day as he was riding a well-trained mount that knew just what to do, the horse stopped for no reason and refused to budge. The leader said, "Walk on" and pulled on the halter, but the horse wouldn't move. The sidewalkers (people who help the child balance in the saddle) all did the same thing with the same result. Finally, the little boy who was still sitting on the horse shouted, "Walk on, Horsie!" The horse immediately obeyed.

So the good news for some horse-loving children who have serious health issues is that they might be able to work with horses. Many kids like Morgan, who has cerebral palsy, and blind Katie (book five) actually can learn to ride! That's because all over the world, people who love horses and children have started therapy riding academies to teach children with special needs how to ride and/or care for a horse. Highly trained horses and special equipment like high-backed saddles with Velcro strips on the fenders make it safe for kids with special needs to become skilled equestrians and thus learn to work with their own handicaps as they never have been able to do before!

A Word about Horse Whispering

If you are constantly reading about horses and know a lot about them, you probably have heard of horse whispering, something that many horse behaviorists do today to train horses. This training process is much different than what the majority of horsemen did several decades ago.

We've all read Wild West stories or seen movies in which the cowpoke "broke" a wild horse by climbing on his back and hanging on while the poor horse bucked until he was so exhausted he could hardly stand. What that type of training did was break the horse's spirit, and the horse learned to obey out of fear. Many "bronco busters" from the past also used whips, ropes, sharp spurs, and painful bits to make the horses respond, which they did only to avoid the pain the trainers caused.

Thankfully, the way many horses become reliable mounts has changed dramatically. Today many horses are trained, not broken. The trainer "communicates" with the horse using herd language. Thus, the horse bonds with his trainer quickly, looks to that person as his herd leader, and is ready to obey every command.

Thanks to Monty Roberts, the "man who listens to horses," and other professional horse whispering trainers like him, most raw or green horses (those that are just learning to respond to tack and a rider) are no longer broken.

Horses are now trained to accept the tack and rider in a short time with proven methods of horse whispering. Usually working in a round pen, the trainer begins by making large movements and noise as a predator would, encouraging the horse to run away. The trainer then gives the horse the choice to flee or bond. Through body language, the trainer asks the horse, "Will you choose me to be your herd leader and follow me?"

Often the horse responds with predictable herd behavior by twitching an ear toward his trainer then by lowering his head and licking to display an element of trust. The trainer mocks the horse's passive body language, turns his back on the horse, and, without eye contact, invites him to come closer. The bonding occurs when the horse chooses to be with the human and walks toward the trainer, thus accepting his leadership and protection.

Horse whispering has become one of the most acceptable, reliable, and humane ways to train horses. Today we have multitudes of rider-and-horse teams that have bonded in such a special way, both the rider and the horse enjoy each other's company. So when you're talking to your friends about horses, always remember to say the horses have been trained, not broken. The word *broken* is part of the horse's past and should remain there forever.

Bible Verses about Horses

Do you know there are about 150 verses in the Bible that include the word *horse*? It seems to me that if God mentioned horses so many times in the Bible, then he is very fond of one of his most beautiful creatures.

Some special verses about horses in the Bible make any horse lover want to shout. Look at this exciting passage from the book of Revelation that tells us about a wonderful time in the future:

"I saw heaven standing open and there before me was a white horse, whose rider is called Faithful and True. With justice he judges and makes war. His eyes are like blazing fire, and on his head are many crowns. He has a name written on him that no one knows but he himself. He is dressed in a robe dipped in blood, and his name is the Word of God. The armies of heaven were following him riding on white horses and dressed in fine linen, white and clean" (Revelation 19:11–14).

The rider who is faithful and true is the Lord Jesus Christ. The armies of heaven on white horses who follow Jesus are those who have accepted him as their Lord and Savior. I've accepted Christ, so I know that some day I'll get to ride a white horse in heaven. Do you think he will be a Lipizzaner, an Andalusian, or an Arabian? Maybe it will be a special new breed of white horses that God is preparing just for that special time.

Perhaps you never realized that there are horses in heaven. Perhaps you never thought about how you could go to heaven when you die. You can try to be as good as gold, but the Bible says that to go to heaven, you must ask Jesus to forgive your sins. Verses to think about: "For all have sinned and fall short of the glory of God" (Romans 3:23); "For God so loved the world that he gave his one and only son, that whoever believes in him shall not perish but have eternal life (John 3:16); "For everyone who calls on the name of the Lord will be saved" (Romans 10:13).

Do you want to be part of Jesus' cavalry in heaven some day? Have you ever asked Jesus to forgive your sins and make you ready for heaven? If you've never done so, please ask Jesus to save your soul today.

As I'm riding my prancing white steed with his long wavy mane and tail dragging to the ground, I'll be looking for you!

Glossary of Gaits

Gait–A gait is the manner of movement; the way a horse goes.

There are four natural or major gaits most horses use: walk, trot, canter, and gallop.

Walk–In the walk, the slowest gait, hooves strike the ground in a four-beat order: right hind hoof, right fore (or front) hoof, left hind hoof, left fore hoof.

Trot–In the trot, hooves strike the ground in diagonals in a one-two beat: right hind and left forefeet together, left hind and right forefeet together.

Canter–The canter is a three-beat gait containing an instant during which all four hooves are off the ground. The foreleg that lands last is called the *lead* leg and seems to point in the direction of the canter.

Gallop–The gallop is the fastest gait. If fast enough, it's a four-beat gait, with each hoof landing separately: right hind hoof, left hind hoof just before right fore hoof, left fore hoof.

Other gaits come naturally to certain breeds or are developed through careful breeding.

Running walk – This smooth gait comes naturally to the Tennessee walking horse. The horse glides between a walk and a trot.

Pace – A two-beat gait, similar to a trot. But instead of legs pairing in diagonals as in the trot, fore and hind legs on one side move together, giving a swaying action.

Slow gait – Four beats, but with swaying from side to side and a prancing effect. The slow gait is one of the gaits used by five-gaited saddle horses. Some call this pace the *stepping pace* or *amble*.

Amble – A slow, easy gait, much like the pace.

Rack – One of the five gaits of the five-gaited American saddle horse, it's a fancy, fast walk. This four-beat gait is faster than the trot and is very hard on the horse.

Jog – A jog is a slow trot, sometimes called a *dogtrot*.

Lope – A slow, easygoing canter, usually referring to a western gait on a horse ridden with loose reins.

Fox trot – An easy gait of short steps in which the horse basically walks in front and trots behind. It's a smooth gait, great for long-distance riding and characteristic of the Missouri fox trotter.

Parts of a Horse

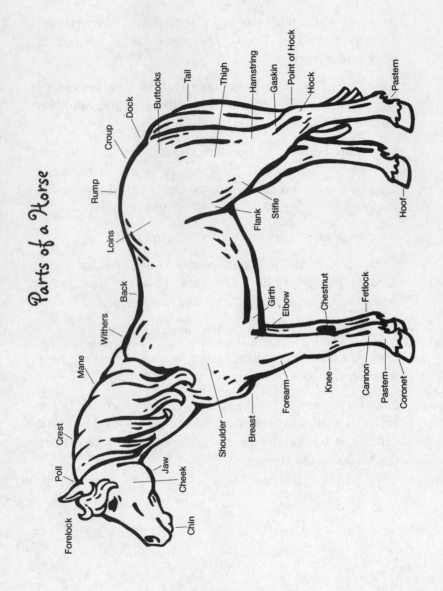

The Western Saddle

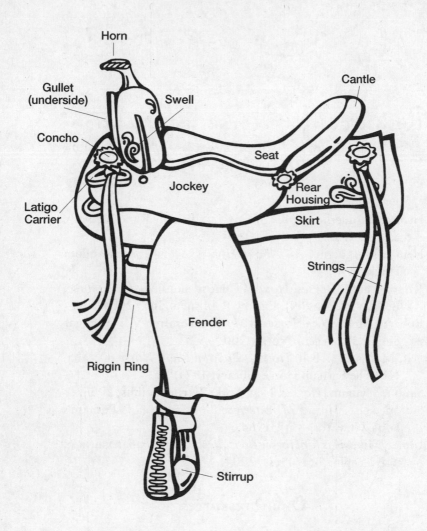

Horn

Gullet
(underside)

Swell

Cantle

Concho

Seat

Jockey

Rear
Housing

Latigo
Carrier

Skirt

Strings

Fender

Riggin Ring

Stirrup

Resources for Horse Information Contained in this Book

Henry, Marguerite. *Album of Horses*. Chicago: Rand McNally & Co., 1952.

Henry, Marguerite. *All About Horses*. New York: Random House, 1967.

Jeffery, Laura. *Horses: How to Choose and Care for a Horse*. Berkley Heights, NJ: Enslow Publishers, Inc., 2004.

Roberts, Monty. *The Horses in My Life*. Pomfret, VT: Trafalgar Square Publishers, North, 2004.

Self, Margaret Cabell. *How to Buy the Right Horse*. Omaha, NE: The Farnam Horse Library, 1971.

Simon, Seymour. *Horses*. New York: HarperCollins, 2006.

Sutton, Felix. *Horses of America*. New York: G.P. Putnam's Sons, New York City, 1964.

Ulmer, Mike. *H is for Horse: An Equestrian Alphabet*. Chelsea, MI: Sleeping Bear Press, 2004.

Online resources

http://www.appaloosayouth.com/index.html
http://www.shetlandminiature.com/kids.asp
http://www.twhbea.com/youth/youthHome.aspx

We want to hear from you. Please send your comments
about this book to us in care of zreview@zondervan.com. Thank you.